The Case *of the*
Stolen Goddess

A Petrie and Pettigrew Novel

John Amos

RIVER GROVE
BOOKS

Published by River Grove Books
Austin, TX
www.rivergrovebooks.com

Distributed by River Grove Books

Design and composition by Greenleaf Book Group
Cover design by Greenleaf Book Group
Cover images used under license from ©Adobestock.com/Valedi;
©Adobestock.com/merfin

Publisher's Cataloging-in-Publication data is available.

Print ISBN: 978-1-63299-813-2

eBook ISBN: 978-1-63299-814-9

First Edition

*To my wife, Sue, as always. To the detectives who struggle
with strange and difficult cases. To the archaeologists who
struggle to restore the ancient past. To T. E. Lawrence and
Gertrude Bell for their cameo appearances. To the memory
of the Ottomans, who held the candle of civilization for
a thousand years. To the bedouin, who have maintained
their honor and tradition in a changing world.
And to everyone else who likes a good story.*

I am Isis, the mistress of every land.
I am the eldest daughter of Cronus,
I am the wife and sister of King Osiris.
I am mother of King Horus,
I am she that rises in the Dog Star,
I am she that is called goddess by women.
—Greek hymn to Isis

To wake in the desert dawn was like
waking in the heart of an opal.
—Gertrude Bell, *The Desert and the Sown*

Contents

Author's Note

This is a story. Any brush with reality is purely accidental. It is written only to allow the imagination to roam freely, unhampered by the cares of the world. In *Henry V*, Shakespeare wrote, "May we cram within this wooden O the very casques that did affright the air at Agincourt?" This story is our wooden O. Add imagination and it expands beyond belief. For it is the imagination that makes us who we are.

Acknowledgments

Editors put up with lots of difficulty. Kitty Walker has put up with more than her share. She has gracefully corrected my faults and calmly replied to my self-doubts. I owe her a debt of gratitude. Ava Koltanovska tutored me on the craft of writing and patiently corrected my many mistakes. This work is much the better because of her wisdom. There are others: Arthur Conan Doyle supplied his unique style of dialogue. Lawrence Durrell added the color and the realism. Ernest Hemingway provided the no-nonsense prose. I stand on the shoulders of giants. The faults are mine; the excellence is theirs.

ONE

The Moon or Six Pence

The statue opened two large blue eyes and smiled at Pettigrew. He was sitting in a garden. The smell of roses was everywhere. Bees buzzed about, and small birds fluttered and chirped in the branches. In front of him was a statue of a woman, all white marble. A gray serpent coiled around her; its head stared at him from under her upraised arm. Its green eyes were cold. The woman nodded at him; she seemed about to speak. Pettigrew leaned forward to listen; the iron bench seat pressed hard against the back of his knees. He began to fall—down, down, down. Time hung motionless as the woman's face blurred and receded into the distance above him. Her smile slowly faded into nothingness. Pettigrew woke up on the floor.

He had fallen out of bed.

Still half-asleep, he went to the window, opened it, and looked out. Warm morning air flooded in, carrying with it the smell of seawater, spices, and cooking meat. He looked down. Below him, men with large turbans and stripped gallabiyahs hurried by; women in black burkas walked slowly, carrying their babies. Donkeys pulled loads of fruit and vegetables. Wagons and carts rattled on the cobblestone. A brown bear with a red hat shuffled by, its trainer a small boy who yelled and hit it with a stick. The bear stood up and pawed the air. Passersby ignored it. Steamers hooted in the Bosporus.

He was back in Istanbul.

Pettigrew closed the window and the hoots stopped. He returned to his bed and pondered on the events that brought him to Istanbul. As he remembered, it had all started with the theft of a statue of Aphrodite on a rainy April evening many months before. But his memory was still bright. The evening was young, the sitting room was warm, and the cognac smelled like burnt caramel. They had been reminiscing about their adventures in Egypt, when they found the lost tomb of Cleopatra.

"We were young then." Flinders picked up two glasses and examined them. "And we didn't know anything."

"Yes, we were lucky to come back alive."

Flinders handed Pettigrew a glass. "Two students, fresh out of Oxford, who thought they could be great detectives."

"That was long ago," Pettigrew said as he sniffed his cognac. "I wonder whatever happened to her."

"You mean Inji?"

"A strange woman." Pettigrew warmed his glass with both hands. "She was someone out of the past."

"Long past."

"But, of course, you couldn't decide whether she was supposed to be your lover or your mother." Pettigrew grinned. "I do have a passing acquaintance with Sophocles, you know."

"So now you have become a Greek playwright."

Flinders took a long sip and stared at his glass. Then he poured a large glass of cognac and handed it to Pettigrew.

"That is a rather full glass, I think," Pettigrew said as he swirled the cognac.

"I gave you three fingers."

"Three fingers? I thought you had five."

"It's an American phrase."

"Ah, yes—no doubt you heard it from the cowboy who bellied up to the bar and drank cactus juice."

"Yes." Flinders poured himself a glass. "He taught me to shoot pistols." Flinders held his glass up to the light. "They were extremely effective when I shot the cultists in Cleopatra's tomb."

"Speaking of tombs . . . as I remember, you said he lived in a tomb and had a dentist for a student."

"Not a tomb—a city."

"And then he left suddenly after an affair in a paddock."

"Americans call it a corral."

"Whatever happened to him?"

"He went back to America and was bushwhacked."

"Bushwhacked?"

"That means he was ambushed and killed."

"Your American friends are very odd, very odd indeed." Pettigrew warmed his glass in both hands. "Flinders, I worry about you. Next you will take to wearing large white hats."

"You have the imagination of a trout."

On that spring night, they had just adjourned from dinner in the dining room after a long day at work. Both were tired. The conversation at dinner had turned to the detective agency and its problems. They finished dinner and were about to make their way to the sitting room down the long hall with its red Azerbaijani runner and playbill of Sarah Bernhardt as Cleopatra on the wall.

"Thomas, I'm bored," Flinders announced, folding his napkin into a careful square and placing it on the table. "We haven't had any excitement since we came back from Egypt, and that was years ago."

"True," Pettigrew replied. He stood and stretched a moment. It had been a long day reading dossiers and police reports, and everything about him felt cramped. "We've been too busy running this business. How many employees have we got? Ten? Twenty? I don't know how many anymore. They all look alike and they're as boring as can be. They are like fish in the London fish market. Their eyes roll at me."

"Not only that, but they don't know what they're doing." Flinders scratched his nose. "I had three of them come and ask me how to follow a miscreant. I told them, 'Just disguise yourselves as greengrocers and carry on.'"

"You were always fond of disguises." Pettigrew chuckled. "You should have become an actor."

"There was one who had some promise." Flinders took a long sip from his glass. "But he left and set up shop somewhere in London."

"You mean that little Belgian who used to be a policeman?" Pettigrew said.

"Yes, a funny little fellow with a huge moustache. He was along in years but very clever. He was always talking about his 'little gray cells.'" Flinders pulled an ear. "I wonder where he went."

"Odd you should ask." Pettigrew smiled. "I met him just the other day at Scotland Yard. I was there looking for information on one of our culprits, and there he was. He has an assistant, a Captain somebody or other. Not the smartest bear in the woods, as I recall."

They left the hall and entered the sitting room. Flinders sat on the silk couch and crossed his knees. Pettigrew watched him as he leaned his head back on the striped cushion. He studied his friend for a moment and then settled into an armchair. He opened the *Times* but was soon distracted— Cleopatra looked down from above the mantelpiece, her brooding eyes hidden in shadow.

Pettigrew looked up from his paper and tried to meet her gaze. "She never changes." He folded the paper, stood up, and put his elbows on the mantel. "Flinders, I still remember the first words Inji said to me in Cairo: 'Do not patronize me, Mr. Pettigrew. I speak several languages, and all of them fluently.'"

"I remember too. I heard her, and I thought you were going to shrivel up and die on the spot."

"Well, you didn't do too well with her either," Pettigrew said with a laugh. "I seem to remember something about scarabs on the floor of the residence. Your eyes had traveled downward, I believe."

"A cat may look at a king," Flinders said as he arched a disdainful eyebrow at Pettigrew.

"You are not a cat, and you should keep your eyes to yourself, especially in the presence of beautiful women."

Flinders also stood and raised his glass. "To Cleopatra."

"To Cleopatra and all that has happened since."

"To all that has happened since."

And all that has happened since.

Pettigrew's mind traveled into the past. The two of them were celebrating their opulence following the success of their work for Lady Stanhope. They had come back from Cairo years before and found themselves feted as the detectives who sought Cleopatra. Headlines had blared: INTREPID DUO BACK FROM SEARCH FOR CLEOPATRA; crowds had waved flags.

Yes, a great deal has happened since.

"Here's to Lady Stanhope." Pettigrew smiled and raised his glass. "To the founder of the feast."

"To Lady Hester," Flinders echoed. "Lady Hester Stanhope." He raised his glass, and Pettigrew watched as the lamplight glimmered through the Medusa face on its stem. The features moved in the flickering light.

Medusa, another representation of female energy. She does not smile; she does not blink. Writhing serpents curl about her head; her eyes could turn a man to stone. What were the ancients thinking when they portrayed her?

Pettigrew raised his glass. "I know she was disappointed when we could not find Cleopatra, but she paid us well anyway." Pettigrew flourished his glass. "But I really think that deep down, she was somehow relieved Cleopatra's body remained hidden. It is too bad that her ladyship died shortly after we returned from Egypt. Well, anyway, now we are famous." He put the glass down. Medusa stared and did not move.

"And well off," added Flinders.

Well off and then some.

"Thomas, think back to all that has happened since we returned."

"Quite a lot. Indeed, quite a lot."

They had started out as eager youths, fresh from Oxford and imbued with Joseph Bell's criminology training. They had rented a flat on Baker Street across from Holmes and Watson. Flinders had proudly hung up a bronze plaque: PETRIE AND PETTIGREW, DETECTIVES. He polished it daily.

Sometimes Pettigrew would come out, watch, and shake his head. Flinders would pace back and forth on Baker Street, the better to view it from different perspectives.

"It's not going to get any larger, you know."

"Ah, but it's the principle it represents."

"Principle, you say?"

"Yes, principle."

"What principle?"

"That we are here and ready to solve any crime."

"But we don't have any crimes yet."

"You really are a dunce."

One morning, when sunlight had just begun to creep down Baker Street and Flinders was pacing, Holmes crossed the cobbles and called out, "What are you doing?"

"I am examining my plaque."

Holmes grinned and pointed at the plaque. "I've watched you putter about this sign for days."

"I like to look at it in the morning when the sun first lights it."

"So you are a poet."

"No, just an ordinary man with a bronze plaque."

Holmes stretched out his hand. "I am Sherlock Holmes."

"I know."

"And whom do I have the pleasure of addressing?"

"I am Flinders Petrie," Flinders said. He shook hands with Holmes. Pettigrew, who had been watching the scene unfold from the top of the steps, came down and joined Flinders and Holmes in the street. He and Flinders stood in the bright sun and faced the great man. A small cat padded by the tableau.

"Petrie—the name is familiar." Holmes shook Flinders's hand. "I know Sir Flinders Petrie, the archaeologist—are you any relation?"

"I am his nephew."

"And you?"

"I am Thomas Pettigrew."

"Ah, Mummy Pettigrew."

"I am his grandson."

"And, like him, you are a physician."

Pettigrew nodded.

"I thought so. You carry yourself like a doctor. I can see ink from medical charts on one hand and calluses from holding a stethoscope on the other."

Holmes smiled and retied the sash of his gray dressing gown with its wide velvet lapels. He turned to Flinders. "And how do you find the museum?"

Flinders jumped in surprise.

Holmes explained. "Your jacket is covered with a particularly dry dust, probably from ancient pieces. Its elbows are worn from rubbing against a table. And your right hand has stains, probably from the wood handle of a magnifying glass. You are clearly a curator of some sort."

The small cat sat down on the steps of the flat.

"Well, well, two chips off the old block," Holmes said merrily. He examined the plaque. A slow smile crinkled his hawklike face. "And now you two are going to be detectives." Holmes's eyes twinkled. "Good luck, my young friends."

He started to turn away and then stopped and faced the two. "Please do come and see us when you need assistance."

He finished the turn and walked back across the street. Watson opened the door. Holmes said something and pointed at the plaque. They both laughed and went inside.

Pettigrew watched the tall, slightly stooped figure go. "An annoying fellow."

"Very."

The small cat lolled on the steps and licked a paw.

Pettigrew quickly found his new life as a detective unrewarding. Finances became an overwhelming problem. Both detectives had to take on other jobs to supplement their income. As Holmes correctly deduced, Flinders became a curator at the British Museum and spent his day pouring over cuneiform tablets. Pettigrew joined a local medical clinic and delivered babies. It was his first experience as a physician.

"The clinic laughs with new life. The mothers smile at me and say, 'Thank you,' but I cannot give their babies life; I can only watch and wonder."

But then Lady Stanhope had arrived, flanked by two large bodyguards, and paid them to find Cleopatra.

And their fortunes had changed dramatically.

They returned from Cairo, hired a manager, and arranged for a triumphal tour. The name "Cleopatra" was on everybody's lips. The new year started with spectacular success, including a tour complete with photographs, costumes, and enactments. Flinders smiled and waved; Pettigrew just stood and scowled.

What am I doing here? I want to be a detective, not a showman.

Even so, the audiences were large and enthralled.

The firm of Petrie and Pettigrew grew into a large detective agency. Uncle Flinders sent them a stream of well-connected clients. Pettigrew Senior opened a pipeline of wealthy mummy collectors. The detectives became well-known figures at the Geographical Society. Famous men shook their hands. They were invited to speak. Flinders delivered lectures. Scholars clapped and cheered. Brandy flowed; backs were slapped.

Pettigrew waited silently in the wings and watched Flinders stand in the circle of light surrounding the podium. Flinders would lecture; Pettigrew would work the magic lantern. Then Flinders would rush off the stage; his face would be alight.

"We could branch out and become famous explorers," Flinders said, pondering the possibilities. "Maybe we should search for the origins of the Nile."

"I think that's already been accomplished." Pettigrew sniffed. "And besides, I can't imagine you trundling about jungles."

After one such lecture, they had gotten into a cab. The engine roared, the exhaust belched, and the cab lurched ahead. After a moment, Flinders turned to Pettigrew.

"Thomas, can't you feel it?" Flinders's eyes were wide; his face was earnest.

"Feel what?"

"I read a story about a village where time did not exist—where the villagers lived forever."

"That is impossible."

"It was in the mountains beyond the horizon."

"There are no mountains beyond the horizon."

"Thomas, there are such mountains, and we must find them. We cannot just polish plaques in Baker Street."

Pettigrew looked at his friend. *Maybe there are horizons beyond the horizon,* he thought. But he answered, "Flinders, you look at the moon and do not see the six pence lying at your feet."

Flinders scowled. "And you see only the six pence. You do not see the moon in its glory."

The cab stopped. The engine ground to a halt, and they got out.

Maggie, their housekeeper, opened the door and beckoned. "Would you like some dessert?"

Photographers sought them out. They smiled as cameras flashed, or at least Flinders did. Pettigrew frowned. He blinked at the flashes.

"We are not celluloid heroes."

"At least try not to stare at the camera."

A young newspaper reporter named Lowell came up to them after one of the lectures. "That was marvelous, and so very fascinating. The audience was enthralled. I thought they would never stop clapping." He took off his wide-brimmed hat and swept it across his chest. "I can make you even more famous. I will write a series of stories about your exploits." He was a short man dressed in baggy clothes.

Pettigrew was not amused. "He seems awfully young," he whispered in Flinders's ear.

"He is eager to make a name for himself," Flinders replied. "Let's hear him out."

"I can photograph you in the desert." Lowell reached into a canvas briefcase. The canvas was stained and torn. "But you will have to pose in costume." He took out some large photographs and shuffled them. "Take a look at these."

Pettigrew peered over his shoulder. The photographs showed men in robes riding camels. The men stared solemnly at the camera. They did not smile.

Lowell looked up. "These are bedouin from the Empty Quarter. They live in the desert. I can photograph you dressed like them and do a series of interviews. Your names will be household words."

Pettigrew examined a photograph. "They look like they are from another world."

It is a world I do not know. A world I don't want to know. It looks harsh and unforgiving.

He shook his head and handed the photograph back. "We should think about this."

"Nonsense."

"But, Flinders, dressed as bedouin?"

"Advertising makes everything happen."

"That's what you said about the lectures."

"Yes, and you were magnificent with the lantern slides."

"Don't you ever have enough?"

"You are a troll."

Flinders invited Lowell to the flat.

Maggie opened the door. "There's a man here with all kinds of equipment. He keeps dropping it on my floor."

"Send him up!" Flinders shouted. "He won't hurt your floor."

"He's too eager."

Lowell began to set up his camera in the sitting room. Flinders watched in delight. "These Americans are wonderful at advertising," he said. Pettigrew rolled his eyes. Lowell opened a leather valise and pulled out some bedouin headdresses.

Flinders smiled. "Now, just look at those."

Pettigrew frowned.

Flinders started rummaging through some gear he had brought back from Cairo. "I know I have a couple of gallabiyahs somewhere."

Lowell took out several curved knives, and Flinders picked up one. "These are just the thing. We can brandish them and smile at the camera. We will look like regular bedouin shaykhs."

That was too much for Pettigrew. "No knives." He glowered. "And no gallabiyahs either."

"You have no imagination."

"We are not going to get dressed up in robes and walk around with large knives."

"All right, no robes, but you have to smile."

"I don't want to smile."

"All right then, be stern." Flinders chuckled. "You look like some ancient pharaoh anyway."

The flashes blazed. Pettigrew stared.

A day later, Lowell rushed back with the photographs. "Look at these! They are wonderful," he said breathlessly. Flinders smiled; Pettigrew frowned.

I see myself in a strange world. But I do not look out of place. How can that be?

One morning, Pettigrew watched while Flinders rummaged through the mail. They had just finished breakfast. The sitting room was quiet. Maggie and Elise murmured in the kitchen below. The dining room clock had just chimed eight, and the morning sun slanted through the white curtains.

"Thomas," Flinders said quite suddenly, "I love the smell of sawdust."

"The smell of sawdust?" Pettigrew put his paper down. "Whatever are you talking about?"

Flinders held up a letter. "This is an offer from Lord Sanger, the circus owner. He wants us to perform an act with camels and elephants. He says that we might become bigger stars than that American, Tom Thumb. Just think, we will be in the hippodrome." Flinders was enthusiastic. "We could travel around the countryside on a circus train."

"Tom Thumb, is it," Pettigrew said with a laugh. "Aren't you a little tall to be playing Tom Thumb?"

"Never mind that. It's the idea, don't you see?"

"So now you want to be in a circus?"

"What excitement!" Flinders danced around the room. "We would be under the big top. We could ride camels."

"I hate camels. We are not going to ride camels."

"Just think of it." Flinders's eyes flashed. "We could parade in the ring. People would throw flowers. Women riding elephants would salute us."

"You ride the elephants—I won't."

But to his dismay, Pettigrew found himself in a cab on the way to the hippodrome. As the cab rolled through the crowded streets, Flinders explained, "Lord Sanger himself will meet us at the entrance. Thomas, we will be famous."

"I don't want to be famous."

"Thomas, just think. I can hear the roar of the crowd now."

"You listen to the crowd; I prefer the silence of our sitting room."

"The band sounds a fanfare." Flinders waxed poetic. "The ringmaster twirls his mustache and doffs his hat. We ride horses into the ring. The clowns do somersaults. The audience cheers."

"Now it's horses and somersaults, is it?"

"Look at these." Flinders unrolled a packet of circus posters and spread them on the cab's seat. "Here are the flyers and wire walkers." He laughed. "Can't you feel the excitement?"

"Those pictures are garish." Pettigrew snorted. "The performers are all distorted. They resemble fish swimming in the air. They look like people from a different universe."

"That may be, but it's a wonderful universe."

"It is an unnatural universe." Pettigrew traced the figures with a finger. "Even a sinister universe."

"You think too much." Flinders unrolled another set. "There is a menagerie; see, this is Jumbo the elephant." He shuffled the papers.

"Wait, what are those?"

"These are the freaks." Flinders waved another poster.

"Let me see those." Pettigrew grabbed a poster. "Samuel, the 'fearless frog boy.' He has shriveled legs and paddles instead of feet." He took another. "Coco, the 'bird girl.' She has no skin, only feathers, and her nose is a beak." He handed the posters back. "Flinders, these are horribly deformed human beings—they belong in a nursing home, not in a sideshow." He leaned back, and the seat felt cold.

A sideshow, a staged production, but what if it became real? He pulled his coat tight around his neck. *What if I found myself in a strange universe where nothing was familiar?* He closed his eyes and rubbed his face. *And what if I had to struggle with horribly deformed creatures? What would I do?*

He opened his eyes and stared out. The sky turned sullen, and rain splashed on the window.

The world turns dark.

The cab splashed to a stop. The hippodrome loomed large and gray in the rain. Colorful posters adorned its stark walls. The images on them postured and leered through trickles of water.

Rain distorts them even more.

Pettigrew and Flinders sat in silence in the cab and watched the rain. The seats became damp; the cab windows clouded.

The darkness surrounds me. Is my world going to fade into such darkness?

The cab's engine idled, a *chug, chug* in the stillness. Raindrops thundered on its roof; its wipers thumped the windscreen in an irregular beat. The two men did not speak.

Finally, Pettigrew turned to Flinders. "This is too much, too terrible. We cannot do this. I know that you want the excitement, but the cost to our souls is too heavy."

"What do you mean?"

"Flinders, these circus people are exhibiting deformity. There is nothing redeeming at all here."

"Deformity, you say?" Flinders closed his eyes. "Let me think."

Pettigrew leaned across the set. "Flinders, we cannot."

"Are you sure?"

"Yes."

Flinders folded the posters. "I was hoping for an adventure. For a chance to show the world who we are." He paused in thought, then sighed, and then nodded slightly. "You may be right. We cannot join this circus."

"Thank you, my friend."

The meeting with Lord Sanger was short.

"We should be immortalized in oil."

Pettigrew buried his head in his newspaper. "Immortalized in oil? Like insects preserved in amber?"

"You know perfectly well what I mean." Flinders traced his fingers along the dining room wall. "Our likenesses belong on walls."

"Like posters of criminals at the London jail?" Pettigrew scratched his nose with the edge of the paper. "Come to think of it, you would look well in stripes."

Pettigrew sighed. The fat birds that flew around the wallpaper paid no attention.

"Our portraits should hang in museums." Flinders struck a pose. "After all, we are the detectives who discovered Cleopatra's tomb."

"Yes, but we didn't tell anybody. Remember?" Pettigrew folded the paper and set it on the varnished dining table. "That was your idea. Some rubbish about Octavian, I think."

"You agreed that Cleopatra should remain a legend."

"I did, and I still do. She cannot be reduced to a shriveled mummy in a museum," Pettigrew said, smiling. "For once, you were right."

"No matter, we are going to have our portraits painted. So practice looking heroic."

"I don't want to look heroic."

"Nonsense. Have you read Carlyle? Heroes make history. Heroes are all the rage."

"I am only a detective. I solve crimes. I do not make history."

Flinders insisted, though, and Pettigrew finally agreed. Flinders had hired a celebrated painter to picture them searching for Cleopatra's tomb. They were to be portrayed as holding torches and peering into a stone doorway as a mysterious light streamed through it. Workmen in fezzes would accompany them.

"This will be marvelous," Flinders said.

"Wait—there were no workers, and the tomb was pitch-black."

"Details. You worry too much."

Flinders thought for a moment. "We will need clothes for the occasion." He left and returned a short time later. "What do you think of this?" He unpacked an elegant sack suit.

"Very nice, indeed." Pettigrew grinned. "But you cannot wear a Bond Street outfit to go into a tomb."

Flinders shook his head and put the suit away. "Some other time." He returned with a large turban. "Perhaps this instead."

"That's four feet across," Pettigrew said. "You look like you're wearing an umbrella." He shook his head. "No turbans."

"You have no sense of style," Flinders said. "Possibly a smaller turban." Then, with an evil smile, he said, "I have one for you as well—you would look marvelous. Like a lovely large cabbage, I think."

"Absolutely not. I will not wear strange headgear."

Once again, Pettigrew found himself in a cab. It stopped in front of a nondescript building. Pettigrew and Flinders entered and climbed a flight of unlit stairs. Voices murmured from below, and the stairwell smelled of cooking. The stair treads squeaked.

Flinders opened an unpainted door. The studio was large and full of paintings, easels, brushes, and tubes of paint. It reeked of linseed oil and mineral spirits. In one corner, a scruffy dog lounged on a blue blanket. A tall man with a goatee and fierce eyes greeted them. He wore a dirty gray smock stained with paint.

"This is John Sargent," Flinders introduced him. "He is very famous."

Sargent bowed and then turned and went over to an easel. "Let me show you my work. Do come and see."

Pettigrew whispered, "Sargent? Is he in the military?"

"No, he's an American."

"That may be worse."

"Be quiet."

The dog rolled over. The blanket was covered with hair.

Sargent lifted the canvas that covered the easel and stood back. "This is my newest painting. I call it *Madame X.* I am thinking of doing something like this with you."

"Wait," Pettigrew said. "Her dress is falling off."

"Indeed so," Sargent said with a grin. "She has a colorful reputation. When her husband sees this, there will be a huge scandal."

Flinders lifted an eyebrow. "A scandal—wonderful!"

Pettigrew sniffed. "I think not. We are serious professionals—our clothes do not fall off."

"Well, then, we'll do something more conventional." Sargent pushed them over to a bench. "Flinders, you sit. Pettigrew, you rest an elbow on his shoulder. Now, do not move."

Sargent pulled an easel over to him and picked up a handful of brushes. "Yes, yes, we will be very solemn." He chewed on a brush; paint dripped on his goatee.

The dog sat up and scratched its ear.

When the painting was finished, Flinders framed it in an ornate gold frame. "The gold gives it an 'old world' feeling," he said. He hung it in the dining room.

Pettigrew studied it. *Two men with dark eyes look solemnly back at me. I can see myself, but I don't recognize that person. I see Flinders, but he is different as well. What was it that Burns wrote? Something about "seeing ourselves as others see us." There is a feeling behind those eyes that Sargent has captured: perhaps an inner trauma that generates a restlessness. We do not move, but we are like caged animals pacing back and forth. I wonder what someone viewing this portrait a hundred years from now would see.*

Pettigrew turned away. *My time is out of joint.*

Famous people invited them to parties. Women in gowns and furs flirted with them; men in tails shook their hands. The invitations continued for years, more so as they became well-known detectives whose faces were often on the front pages for having solved an intractable crime. Petrie and Pettigrew had become household names as the detectives deluxe.

As late as the month before, a young American actress came up to them at a soiree. Soft yellow lamps swung overhead. Jazz music wailed from the stage. Couples danced in the flickering light; perfume wreathed the dancers. She was a small woman with heavy-lidded eyes darkened by mascara.

Flinders shook her hand. Pettigrew frowned.

She blushed and said, "My name is Theda. I act in films. I have come to England just to see you." She smiled. "They call me 'the vamp.'" She smiled again. "But you have inspired me to create the role of Cleopatra."

Flinders asked her how he and Pettigrew could help. Perhaps they could travel to Hollywood to act as advisers? Possibly even as actors like that Rathbone fellow?

Flinders offered her his arm. "May I get you some champagne?"

"Yes, thank you. Let me use the powder room, and I'll be right back."

Flinders bowed and then watched her go.

"Flinders, what are you getting us into?" Pettigrew growled when she was out of earshot. "She's almost half your age."

"Nonsense. Young women find older men with a touch of salt and pepper in their hair tremendously attractive." Flinders smoothed his hair.

"You'd be robbing the cradle."

"You're becoming a boring old trollop." Flinders signaled to the waiter. "Some champagne, please."

"We are detectives, not actors. We have a reputation to uphold."

"Yes, but we are also men of the world." Flinders took two glasses of champagne from the waiter's tray. "We must encourage the arts."

"The arts? What are you talking about? Flinders, sometimes I wonder about you."

"You have no soul."

"You are becoming an overage lecher."

"Ah, here she comes." Flinders smiled and extended a glass. "Do have some champagne, my dear."

She smiled and accepted the glass. Flinders offered her his arm. As they walked off, arm in arm, Flinders turned, arched an eyebrow, and whispered to Pettigrew, "The silver screen beckons."

The band struck up "Come Josephine, in My Flying Machine," and Flinders led Theda onto the dance floor.

Pettigrew shrugged and reached for another glass of champagne.

TWO

The Far Pavilions Call

Over the years, Flinders charmed his hosts; Pettigrew remained largely silent. Onlookers took his silence to be an air of mystery. Newspaper reporters likened him to some ancient pharaoh, something from the exotic Middle East. "A new Thutmose," they said. But it was not an air of mystery; he was just shy and socially awkward.

When they returned to the flat after an outing, Flinders would often lecture Pettigrew. "Thomas, you have to smile and say something."

"I don't want to—these people are silly."

"Silly or not, you have to be pleasant."

"Rubbish."

"Rubbish or not, you must be congenial." Flinders thought for a moment. "I have it!" He pulled Pettigrew to the mirror in the dining room. "Let's practice smiling. Watch, it's not difficult. Even you can master it." Flinders grinned. "That may take some time, of course."

Flinders stood next to Pettigrew and smiled at the mirror. "See, how easy? Now you try it."

Pettigrew managed a limp smile.

Flinders clapped his hand to his brow. "No, no, no, not like that. That's not a smile; that's a drool." He turned away and shrugged his shoulders. "I give up." He reached for the decanter. "Maybe we should try acting lessons." He poured a glass and stared through its amber depths and muttered, "Maybe the *Opera Comique*."

"Thomas, do you think that we should become actors?"

"Actors, is it?" Pettigrew was surprised. "I thought you practiced disguising yourself already."

"That is what good detectives do." Flinders smiled. "Think of Holmes. Holmes was a masterful actor. He used disguises in many of his cases."

"Indeed."

Flinders thought for a moment. "Thomas, did I ever tell you about the time Holmes and I went to pubs?"

Pettigrew shook his head.

"It was a few years after we came back from Egypt. I think that you were away at some kind of medical convention at the time." Flinders laughed. "Holmes and I met in the street. I was disguised as a pensioner because I was helping the Metropolitan police find the White Chapel murderer. Holmes was disguised as an old woman."

"So?"

"But his elbows were wrong. You cannot disguise elbows, and he should have covered them. I said, 'Mr. Holmes, I presume.' He jumped and looked, and then he laughed and said, 'Good show, young man, but your walk is off.' He saw right through my costume."

"I'm not surprised."

"He said that he was searching for a beggar with a twisted lip."

"A twisted lip?" Pettigrew shook his head. "You mean a harelip. Why was the beggar disguised like that? Was he an actor playing the part of Caliban?"

"No, he disguised himself that way because he knew no one would look closely at a deformed person."

"But you told me that everyone wanted to see the freaks at Sanger's hippodrome. And they were horribly deformed."

"That is different."

"I see."

Flinders changed the topic. "Holmes said that he quite often used disguise. One thing led to another. We made a bet to see who could create the most believable disguise. We went to pubs to see if anyone could recognize us. His disguises were incredible. I never could get the best of him."

"As I remember, there were some evenings when you came home smelling quite strongly of beer."

"Never mind that. Thomas, you must learn to act and be friendly."

"So now you want me to become an actor like that fellow in *The Prisoner of Zenda*?"

"Come to think of it," Flinders said with a chuckle, "you would be magnificent as Rupert of Hentzau."

"The villain?"

"But of course."

"Rubbish," Pettigrew muttered to himself as he walked down the hall and into the sitting room. Sarah Bernhardt smiled at him from her poster. He looked back at her.

They all smile.

"Still rubbish."

Women wrote love letters to Flinders. They did not write letters to Pettigrew. Every morning, Maggie brought up piles of envelopes and placed them on a chinoiserie table in the sitting room. The table often overflowed; letters spilled onto the floor. Some were stained with lip rouge; others smelled strongly of perfume.

"Flinders, this is getting outrageous," Pettigrew said one day, when he found Flinders on the couch, surrounded by torn-open envelopes. "Who gave all these women our postal number?"

Flinders just smiled and continued to open envelopes. Some he simply read; others he stopped and considered.

Pettigrew glowered, took a chair next to Flinders, and loudly opened a newspaper.

"Are you all right?" Flinders was unfazed. "You seem disturbed. Perhaps some brandy." He opened another letter and sniffed loudly.

Pettigrew frowned. "Now what are you doing?"

"Research."

"Research?"

"Etoile de Amour." Flinders sniffed the envelope. "A truly elegant scent." He looked thoughtful for a moment. "From an older woman, I think. One who is sure of herself."

"So you have become an expert in French perfume," Pettigrew growled. "And now you deduce a woman's character from her perfume."

"But of course. A woman chooses her perfume to enhance her self-image."

"A waste of time. For her *and* for you."

"A detective must be knowledgeable in all things." Flinders picked up another envelope. "Remember, Holmes spent years studying cigar ashes." He opened it. "I believe that he examined 243 different types."

"But perfume?"

"Women do commit crimes, you know." Flinders paused. "Surely you remember Amelia Dyer, the nurse who murdered all those infants. She was particularly fond of lavender oil. All the dead infants smelled of it. That's how the police caught her."

Flinders reached for another envelope.

"Give me that." Pettigrew snatched the envelope. "This smells terrible."

Flinders snatched it back. "You have no soul. No imagination."

Pettigrew shook his head.

"A gentleman must be educated in these matters." Flinders shook the envelope. "How many times have I counseled you on your lack of social skills?" He tapped his forehead. "How many times? How many years? Distressing. Truly distressing."

"That's not quite fair."

"It is fair."

"We get plenty of mail that is enjoyable and appeals to our higher sensibilities."

"Higher sensibilities? You sound like a missionary." Flinders frowned behind an envelope. "You are a dull fellow and miss the sublime things in life."

"A missionary?"

"Yes, you are like those terrible ladies in straw hats, singing and beating drums. You march around preaching; you are always looking at your boots. You must look up to see the sky."

"I see."

"No, you don't." Flinders put the envelope down and stretched forward on the couch. "Thomas, if we look up, we can write our will across the stars."

"Maybe so, maybe not."

Pettigrew folded his newspaper and reached for a stack of unopened letters.

"Flinders, did you see this letter?" he said, after quickly skimming through a few that were of no interest. "It is from a young Catholic priest who wants to become a detective. Father Brown, or something like that. He is very sly; no one expects a priest to be a sleuth. He wants our advice."

"Then give him some advice."

"What kind of advice do you give a priest?"

"That is your problem, not mine."

Flinders shuffled through the rest of the mail. "Aha! Fleurs de France, an excellent perfume."

"You seem very pleased with yourself."

"The world is our oyster." Flinders poured himself another glass.

"An oyster, you say." Pettigrew joined him.

The glasses clinked.

"An oyster full of pearls."

"Indeed."

And indeed it was. Or so it seemed.

Their flat had been refashioned; the old couch and chairs were replaced by Napoleon III–style gold-encrusted furniture with silk brocade coverings. Flinders had proclaimed, "That old Louis XV stuff is out of date; Belle Epoque is the vogue now." And he had set about ordering new furniture. Pettigrew had shrugged and left him to it.

Pettigrew looked about the room. He grudgingly admitted that Flinders had applied some elegant touches. The once-bare floor now sported a red

Persian Sultanabad, and the wall over the small fireplace now held a large painting of Cleopatra.

"Something of a splurge," Flinders had put it, as he admired the painting—Pettigrew had been the one to hang it—"but it sets off the decor perfectly."

Pettigrew often muttered something about how he never knew what he would see when he opened the door to the flat.

In the corner of the room, just left of the fireplace, a large bronze bust of Isis stood on a pedestal: a beautiful woman entwined by a serpent. Pettigrew had discovered it in the London art market and snapped it up at once. Isis smiled from her pedestal, while the serpent remained expressionless. Its eyes glittered with a cold, empty stare.

Maggie carefully dusted Isis every day.

But not everything was changed in the drive to be *au courant* that had taken hold of Flinders. The small dining room was much the same. Flinders had originally wallpapered it in fat birds with puffy red beaks that flew endlessly around the room. The fat birds had survived multiple redecorations. Often Flinders would pat the birds and say, "They belong here. They are like us, always flying." A small oak table with chairs sat in the middle of the room. A walnut hunt bar stood along one wall. Flinders had found a crystal decanter and glasses with Medusa head decorations and placed them with great ceremony on the bar. "Elegant crystal is the mark of gentlemen." Maggie carefully kept the decanter filled with cognac.

But the decorating changes were not all.

Maggie continued serving mutton, but now Pettigrew requested that she serve him hummus as well. He ate it with unleavened bread. Once Maggie had suggested that perhaps with some curried onions and peppers, it would taste better.

"No, I want it served just as it was served in Cairo."

I want to remember the woman I loved. We ate hummus together before she died. The flavor brings back the memory.

Maggie had objected, saying that hummus was foreign food, not healthy at all, and hard to find. "You have become very strange at times since you came back from Egypt," she huffed, "but I know of a Syrian green grocery, and I will do as you ask. But you should eat only manly English food. Mutton is manly—that is what's good for you, so eat your mutton."

One morning, shortly after their return from Egypt, Maggie came upstairs and asked if they would care to interview a young woman—a woman Maggie said was an excellent baker and could help out with the cooking and other duties.

"Since you are now famous detectives, you should eat better meals," Maggie declared. "I have found a wonderful helper; her name is Elise. I have thought about it, and here is what is to be done. We will acquire two more rooms from the flat across the way and have a carpenter make a door in the back hallway. That way, both Elise and I will have more room, and you will have the service you deserve." She folded her arms and stood back expectantly.

And so it was. Pettigrew started to say something, but Flinders had already taken Maggie's suggestion. "A brilliant idea," he said.

Pettigrew assumed Maggie's excitement had to do with the fact that she would no longer be alone in her quarters.

Her life must be lonely, much like mine.

"And it will be nice for you to have a companion," he added simply.

The young woman turned out to be the granddaughter of Dora, with whom Maggie had worked years before, when she was housekeeper to a general.

"Dora was a superb baker of French pastries—the general loved them, and you will love them," Maggie had proclaimed when the girl arrived and stood shyly in the parlor for introductions. "Elise was taught to bake by her mother. You have hired a baking dynasty."

After a few desserts, both men agreed that the new hire was indeed remarkable, even without a baking dynasty.

In addition to the two new rooms, a small garden had been added at the rear of the building. Flinders filled it with white wrought-iron furniture adorned with the face of Jenny Lind, the "Swedish Nightingale."

"I got the idea from the American, Barnum. He put her face everywhere."

Pettigrew grinned. "Next you will be figuring out how to put our faces on iron benches."

"You might have something there."

There were a number of plants—roses and honeysuckle—and a small sphinx. The sphinx was a gift from Uncle Flinders; it had a woman's face and a long tail. The tail curled around its back. Flinders had named it Matilda in honor of his uncle's sometime betrothed. The sphinx did not smile. The garden smelled of flowers.

In the mornings, when the dew was still fresh, Flinders would sit in the garden and read the mail and admire the sphinx. Pettigrew would look down from his bedroom window and see him sitting on the wrought-iron bench, and sometimes Pettigrew envied Flinders for his ability to be completely at ease in every moment.

Once, upon returning from his garden meditations and reflections, Flinders told Pettigrew that sometimes he let his imagination run and would see a small girl riding on the sphinx.

"I imagined that she laughed and that she smiled at me." He looked thoughtful for a moment and then added, "Thomas, I remember what another woman said years before." His voice was quiet. "She sat next to me in the railway car and said, 'I had a dream. I saw white marble and red columns, and fountains splashing. There was a sphinx; I used to ride on it.'"

Pettigrew had smiled and nodded. He, too, remembered what had happened in Egypt and the woman who had the dream.

Neither of us will ever forget her, he thought.

For a while, Pettigrew felt that everything had worked out as it should in their lives. They were older now; they were content. But there was angst—an emotion that neither could express. At least Pettigrew's expectations had always been realistic. Flinders was another matter.

They had enough cases to keep them busy. And their reputations as detectives had grown. But then a yearning set in—a yearning for something greater than their comfortable world. A yearning for action. Pettigrew missed the excitement of their earlier adventures, and he sensed that Flinders did too. Not *sensed*—Flinders's restlessness made it obvious. Time began to drag; the two fretted about the flat. Flinders rearranged the furniture; Pettigrew puttered with medical journals. Months passed; hope faded.

What had they become? Two aging men with nothing left but memories of the past and fantasies of the future.

What was it Shakespeare wrote? "Tomorrow, and tomorrow, and tomorrow, creeps in this petty pace from day to day."

The days went on without end, and the nights were often without sleep.

Maggie rattled in the kitchen; the sound returned Pettigrew to the present. The sitting room slowly darkened as the sun set somewhere beyond the windowpanes, and the city itself grew quiet. Pettigrew lit the gas lamps. Their light flickered on the portrait. Cleopatra's eyes seemed to move. Pettigrew thought her eyes sought him out.

She reaches out from centuries past. She reminds me of the weight of time.

"It was a good run, but there must be more," Flinders said and stared into his glass. "Thomas, I yearn for the far pavilions, for the horizons lost in time."

Pettigrew sighed. "For the far pavilions?" he asked.

The far pavilions. I do know what he means. The place behind the sunset. The place where time ends, and adventure begins. But is it truly possible to go there?

"Yes, for the horizons beyond the horizon."

"You are a middle-aged man."

"That does not matter."

"Your Irish blood has gotten out of hand," Pettigrew said gently. "Perhaps you should adjourn to a Turkish bath for amusement."

"Strange, I thought I saw a copy of Burton's *Pilgrimage to Meccah* on your bedside table." Flinders laughed. "Perhaps you have a secret yearning also."

"I was doing research."

I was imagining.

"Of course you were."

"You may be right," Pettigrew said with a laugh. "We are like old war-horses, stomping and pawing the ground and waiting for the bugle to sound the charge." His brow wrinkled. "But there may be no charge. We are expected to be businessmen now." He closed his newspaper. "The world has changed. No one wants a pair of adventurers now. The world wants men in suits, carrying notebooks and discussing figures."

"I agree. There are no more Lady Stanhopes with their sabers and their maps. They have been left in the dust of progress." Flinders stood up from the sofa and began to pace. "And perhaps we have been left in the dust also."

"But now we are famous detectives."

"So was Holmes, and look what happened to him. He became a caricature, a predictable figure, an unchanging figment of Watson's imagination."

"There may yet be hope."

"A miracle, perhaps."

"It has been an eventful time," Pettigrew said and put the crystal head stopper back in the decanter. Its Medusa eyes stared unblinking at him.

Flinders finished his glass. The fireplace was aflame. Cleopatra pouted; Isis smiled. The glasses were empty. The sitting room was quiet. Flinders paced back and forth and finally went to the window. He pulled the curtains aside, turned briefly to where Pettigrew sat reading, and then turned back to the pane. His restlessness was tangible, a solid thing.

"It looks like rain," he said.

Pettigrew looked down at his newspaper, but nothing in it caught his interest. A dish rattled in the kitchen.

"Although things are going splendidly, we could still use another big case," Flinders growled as he stared into the silent street. The street lamps were on, and the evening fog had begun to creep between the buildings. Shadows interspersed with yellow streams from the lamps stretched like long fingers across the cobbles. Pettigrew could see their reflection from where he sat. Flinders's silhouette was outlined by black and yellow hues as he scrubbed the window's cloudy surface.

I wonder what he sees when he looks out. Does he see far pavilions dancing in the sun? When I look out, I see a dark and dreary street.

Flinders pulled the curtain wider. "I see that Holmes and Watson appear to have a new client."

"And, of course, you imagine that they will get an exotic case," Pettigrew folded his newspaper, "but the truth is that the case they get will be more of the same: a jealous husband, a conniving aunt, or a murder in an idyllic country village." He pulled the decanter's stopper and poured another glass. "No doubt it will be a case where village priests run everywhere. Idyllic but boring."

I've become a middle-aged cynic.

Medusa remained unsmiling.

"Well, maybe not this time." Flinders scrubbed at the window in earnest. "This one looks to be very professional—like that diplomat in the Bohemian scandal." Flinders spread the curtains wider. "A woman was involved in that case. What was her name? An opera singer. Adler, I think. Holmes was much taken with her."

"Adler. You are right. There is much more to Holmes than Watson lets on. We misjudged him once." Pettigrew put the newspaper down. "Holmes loved the puzzle, the chase, and the capture. We are great rivals, but we are kindred spirits."

"Wait!" Flinders let go of the curtains. "He's not going to see Holmes and Watson. He may be coming this way."

A large, well-dressed man had stepped out of a shiny black Daimler, opened an umbrella, crossed the sidewalk, and climbed the short flight of steps. He knocked on the front door. Flinders pulled the white curtains aside for a better look. The door opened; a woman came out, and there was a short conversation. Then she pointed. The man went back down the steps and started to walk across the street below. He looked up at the flat.

"Thomas, hide the cognac," Flinders said, turning away from the window in some excitement. "We are about to have a visitor."

Flinders retied the sash on his purple brocade lounging robe with its wide fur collar and pulled down the cuffs of his white shirt with their scarab cufflinks. Pettigrew buttoned his chalk-striped gray smoking jacket, straightened his green silk cravat, and knocked the ashes out of his pipe. Pettigrew's old paisley smoking jacket and Flinders's plain robe were long gone; they were now replaced by sartorial splendor.

"Quick now, look professional."

Pettigrew stood, arms folded, by the window; Flinders moved toward the door and placed his hand on the nearby mantel. Both looked stern.

A very impressive tableau, thought Pettigrew, *one worthy of Holmes himself.*

Moments later, Maggie brought the man upstairs. He was tall, with graying hair and a neat gray mustache.

"My name is E. A. Wallis Budge," he said as he extended his hand, "but you may call me Wallis. I met you in Cairo a few years ago. I helped you translate some old texts. My assistant, Helen, was killed by the cultists. I found her in the palace basement. She had been strangled most brutally. Her loss was a great blow." His face clouded and he mumbled almost to himself. "A very great blow, indeed."

Both detectives nodded and shook Budge's hand.

Flinders said, "We are sorry for your loss; she must have been a great friend to you. Do come in and sit down." He led Budge to a seat on the dark red Napoleon III couch.

Budge surveyed the room. He had the eye of a hawk. He took a seat on the couch; he moved slowly, as though he were carrying a heavy weight.

I remember how Flinders described him when he spoke about the feud between Budge and his uncle. What did Flinders say? "Budge climbed over the backs of everyone: he was arrogant and aggressive."

Pettigrew studied Budge. He had not changed much since their time in Egypt. His short, cropped hair, once brown, was now gray with white streaks. He was heavier, with the expansive waist of a successful museum director. His pince-nez had been exchanged for the rimless spectacles, and the tweedy jacket with leather elbow patches was now a silky gray Saville Row pinstripe. But the alertness and the preciseness were still there. Pettigrew thought a moment. He had read about the irregularities at the British Museum, where "collectors" were selling the museum artifacts at inflated prices, and he wondered at Budge's svelte appearance.

This is a hard man. He has the coldness of a man who has fought his way up, he thought. *I wonder if there is anyone or anything that he cares about. I did not like him in Cairo, and I am not sure that I care for him now. But still, there may be more to him than I thought.*

"You must be young Flinders," Budge noted. "You've changed." He looked intently at Flinders. "You have put on some weight; now you look very impressive. And Doctor Pettigrew, how nice to see you again. But tell me, what ever happened to that beautiful Egyptian woman—I believe her name was Inji? She was Lord Cromer's assistant. I have thought about her quite a lot over the years." Budge stroked his chin. "It was almost as though she was from another time. In fact, I consulted with other members of the Ghost Club to see if she were related to some ancient deity . . . Isis, perhaps."

Yes, from another time. In his mind, Pettigrew saw Inji's dark eyes and full lips. *How could anyone not remember her? When I first saw her, I thought I had never seen a more beautiful woman. But there was a timelessness about her; I could not place it. She sat in front of Budge and purred like a kitten. He was helpless. While I watched, I thought, "That must have been the way Cleopatra seduced Caesar." Caesar didn't have a chance either.*

Flinders pulled up a green-striped bergère and sat down. "It has been a few years, but we are glad to see you again. Your translation of the Coptic texts was truly masterful and helped us immensely."

Budge smiled and made a slight bow. The couch creaked as he moved.

"Would you care for some tea? Or perhaps a cognac?" Flinders was the consummate host.

"Cognac, please."

Flinders retrieved the cognac, poured a glass, and set it before Budge.

Pettigrew lounged by the window and watched Budge. He was agitated about something, perhaps something more than just his assistant's brutal murder; his hands shook imperceptibly. The cognac spilled as he raised his glass.

I hope he does not want us to help him with another libel action. He has had so many of them.

Budge put his spectacles in a small case. He finished the cognac. Pettigrew continued to watch him. Flinders knew about him from his uncle, but what was it Flinders had said? Something about Budge being a very controversial man. Born to a working-class family and self-educated, he had risen to the position of Keeper of Antiquities at the museum. He had used his position to expand the museum's antiquity holdings and became wealthy in the process. He had engaged in a spectacular feud with Sir Flinders Petrie about the origins of the Egyptians. He was a brilliant raconteur and a much sought-after dinner guest.

Curious, indeed, Pettigrew thought. He turned back to the window and put his hands on its ledge. *And now he sits here with his hat in his hand.*

Budge wiped his lips with a large handkerchief.

"Normally, I would not dream of talking to you again, but this is an emergency, and I am at my wit's end."

Flinders refilled his glass, and Budge took a sip. "May I speak freely?"

The detectives nodded.

"Your uncle and I are sworn enemies, but your reputation is all over the Geographical Society," he continued, his voice lowered. "And I badly need some expert help. I tried retaining Holmes and Watson, but they are semi-retired and are not taking any new cases. Other detectives refuse to leave England if the case were to take them outside of the country."

I am not surprised. Pettigrew was skeptical. *It may be that they simply refused to accept him as a client. He is a man with a checkered history. And a reputation for stinginess.*

Budge took a sip. "You are the only detectives with expertise in the Middle East."

Pettigrew glanced at Flinders and muttered under his breath, "I told you so."

Flinders agreed. "Yes, Holmes never really recovered from the Reichenbach Falls incident. He took up beekeeping in Sussex and comes to London only twice a month. Watson is now married, but he has heart problems and does not go out as much. However, we are at your service. And I must say that you haven't aged a moment. I can see why Inji was so taken with you."

But he had aged. Pettigrew could see the worry lines in his face.

"Yes, yes, a striking woman." Budge smiled and then frowned. "But now I am the head curator of the British Museum, and there has been a terrible theft. A small statue of Aphrodite has been stolen from the Elgin Collection, and I suspect that it has been transferred to some private collector."

"A private collector?" said Pettigrew. "Curious. Who can afford these things?"

"The statue is one of the premier pieces of the collection, second only to the marbles. Its loss is incalculable." Budge paused and then added, "I used to go after these thieves myself, but now my duties make that impossible."

Flinders arched an eyebrow. "So you have come to us?"

"You are the only ones."

"We are the only ones?" Pettigrew said. "There must be others. What about the little detective with the big mustache? He has been in the Middle East."

"I talked to him, but quite frankly, I want somebody younger." Budge's small mustache drooped. "I was disappointed in what he had to offer." Budge frowned. "He did not appear to be a man of action. I think he preferred to solve crimes in his sitting room. And that assistant of his." Budge rolled his eyes. "My goodness."

"Ah, the good captain again. So you have come to us?" Flinders arched an eyebrow.

Pettigrew listened. *Clearly, we are his only option. But do we want his case? We need to know more.*

"We will be happy to do anything to help," Flinders said, "and we will be very discrete, if you understand what I mean."

Not so fast, thought Pettigrew, but Budge looked relieved, so Pettigrew said nothing.

"Good," said Budge. "The museum will pay you well. I understand that you want a retainer, some expense money, and then you will bill by the day." He pulled out a large black checkbook embossed with the museum's logo and wrote a draft.

Pettigrew took the draft, studied it, and then said, "These are the old rates. We charge a little more now, but no matter—we will catch up the difference later." He carefully folded the draft and put it on the mantel. "This can wait."

Flinders smiled in approval.

Crocodile leather, Pettigrew thought, eyeing the checkbook. *Very expensive for a museum director. I see a gold watch fob chain. Yes, he has done very well indeed. But at what cost?*

"Can you tell us something about the theft?" Flinders asked. "Whatever you can think of that might be relevant and useful to us."

Budge lifted the small leather briefcase that rested at his feet and set it on the coffee table. He studied it for a moment before opening it.

"As you know," he began, "the museum has a large collection of Greek marbles. The Parthenon Marbles are the most famous. Lord Elgin acquired them along with several other sculptures in the early 1800s. He claimed that the works had been given to him by a firman—a decree—from the Ottoman sultan. The collection is housed in a special wing of the museum." He took another sip of his cognac.

"Please do go on," Pettigrew said.

"Yes. Well, there are other marbles in that wing. Yesterday, someone broke into the museum, smashed a case, and took a statue of Aphrodite. The thief even got by Mike, the museum's guard cat. He makes quite a racket if anything is amiss. The sound of broken glass alone would have set him off. Mike has been guarding the museum for over ten years. I brought him in; the staff loves him. But the statue is small and easily carried; someone could have hidden it in a large pocket. It was sculpted by Praxiteles as a model for his larger work, the *Aphrodite of Knidos.*"

"Could you explain? Why was it so small? I thought Praxiteles only sculpted large works."

"Sculptors often make small models, called maquettes, to use as working guides. They are used in the same way that painters use preliminary sketches. Usually, maquettes are made of clay or alabaster so that they can easily be changed as needed." Budge shook his head. "But this small Aphrodite is made of marble and has the exact proportions as its life-size sister, and it is priceless."

"How so?" Pettigrew asked.

"Praxiteles originally sculpted Aphrodite as a cult figure. The statue was considered the perfect depiction of the female form and was widely copied." Budge stood and poured himself another glass and then sat back down. "The completed, full-size sculpture was placed in the temple at Knidos but was destroyed sometime in the fourth century. Nothing remains of the original except the maquette." Budge took a large gulp. "But the maquette is unique because it depicts Aphrodite as a woman in a serpent's coil. Praxiteles drew on the Isis myth to depict it." Budge suddenly looked forlorn. "Its loss is catastrophic."

The Isis myth again. Pettigrew looked at the bust of Isis on her pedestal. *You will haunt us forever.*

Isis smiled back.

Budge put his head in his hands. He took another long swallow; the cognac made a ring on the table when he put it down.

"I bought the miniature original in Damascus. I was on a tour to acquire antiquities. The man who sold it to me was an Ottoman general. He said that it had been given to his family, along with a large *mulk*—a land grant—by Sultan Abdul Majid I for their services in the Crimea. He showed me the firman from the sultan: it had the *tughra*—the official signature—of Abdul Majid."

"Let me be clear . . ." Flinders said, pausing and frowning. Pettigrew could see Flinders was not happy with Budge's narrative. "You bought a statue of Aphrodite in Damascus from an old Ottoman general." Flinders folded his arms. "An original by Praxiteles? A priceless treasure? Correct?" Flinders rubbed his chin. "These things do not just float around in bazaars."

"No, no, that was not the case," Budge said, his tone defensive. "I had an expert in Greek sculpture examine it. He pronounced it authentic."

Flinders steepled his hands. "My late uncle said that he could produce one of these 'artifacts' a month. Do you have a provenance?"

"Yes." Budge frowned. "I am . . ." Then he laughed. "I am fully aware of your uncle's creative skills. He even got the museum to accept one of his 'finds.' But this was not the case. I took care to investigate. Great care. And yes, there was a provenance."

"Good."

"I was skeptical of the firman, so I brought in an Ottoman expert to check it for authenticity. He examined the firman and the tughra and said that they were both authentic. The family had fallen on hard times and needed to sell the statue. I personally authenticated the piece and purchased it for the museum."

"Then you are sure that what you want us to recover is the real thing?"

"I am."

"A statue of Aphrodite that harks back to Isis and before?"

"I am aware of its meaning."

Flinders frowned. "We need to think about this." He looked at Pettigrew. "Do you remember Lady Hester?"

"Yes, we were young then, but now . . ." Pettigrew shook his head.

"Thomas, there is nothing to think about."

I can see the far pavilions dance before your eyes, but we need to make sure.

Pettigrew folded his arms. "Director Budge, you are asking us to recover a statue of an ancient woman. That is a difficult task. You must tell us more."

There was silence.

The fat birds paused mid-flight in the dining room. Somewhere, a clock chimed. Maggie and Elise murmured below. Dust motes circled lazily in the air. Raindrops pattered on the window. The sitting room was bathed in breathless shadow.

Then Budge nodded. "Anything you need."

Pettigrew went to the window and looked out at the streetlamps. Their yellow lights created hazy circles in the rain. The anxious face of Budge was reflected in the window. Flinders's face was barely visible in the shadow behind Budge. Their faces wavered and changed colors in the window's shifting light. Pettigrew stared down at the street below for a moment and then closed the curtains and nodded at Flinders.

"Far pavilions it is."

He left the window, went to the mantel, and picked up the check. "You do understand that we may not be able to recover the statue?"

Budge nodded. "Yes."

"And you still wish us to proceed?"

"Yes."

"We will take your case." Pettigrew put the check in his pocket and returned to the window.

Flinders sat back in his chair, crossed his knees, and carefully pulled up a trouser at the knee. He reached into a pocket, pulled out a worn note-book, and began to write. "Please tell us what happened. Do not leave any details out."

Budge sighed and dabbed an eye with his handkerchief. He put on his spectacles; the lenses were fogged.

Crocodile tears to match crocodile leather, thought Pettigrew. *He is going to lie to us—I feel it in my bones.*

"The Aphrodite has been on display for almost twenty years. She is a marvelous piece; your heart would melt if you saw her. She is incredibly beautiful." Budge took off his glasses and wiped his eyes. "I am sorry, but the loss of such beauty is heartbreaking; the world deserves to see it. It should never be hidden away in some rich collector's mansion."

This is nonsense. He just wants his statue back. There is no need for this melodrama.

"Could you be more precise?" Flinders leaned forward. "For example, how tall was the statue?"

"Not tall—possibly twelve inches high."

Flinders scratched an ear with his pen. "You think that some collector broke into the British Museum just to steal one small statue?"

"I do not know."

"I do not think so."

Pettigrew turned to Flinders and shrugged. "There must be some other reason. I think that there is more to this story than we know."

Flinders nodded. "I take it there are witnesses?" he asked. "At least a guard or custodian who heard something?"

"No, no one saw anything," Budge said unhappily, looking up at the ceiling. "The gallery was empty. It had been closed for cleaning."

I think he is lying. But why?

"So no one saw anything, but a priceless statue has disappeared?" Pettigrew asked.

Flinders looked at Pettigrew but said nothing.

Budge also remained silent.

"We will want to talk to your staff, anyway," Pettigrew insisted. "It is possible that someone saw the culprit."

"I can gather the staff."

Pettigrew frowned. "We will need to examine the location of the robbery as soon as possible. I take it you have preserved the scene?"

"Yes, yes." Budge took a large swallow of his cognac. "I locked down the entire wing immediately. No one has entered since last night."

"Then we must go at once." Pettigrew stood up. "We will follow your car."

Budge left the room; the door closed behind him. Flinders arched an eyebrow. Pettigrew grinned. The two pulled on jackets and turned to follow Budge.

"Where are the overcoats?" asked Flinders. "It is raining."

"Never mind the overcoats right now." Pettigrew opened the dining room door and shouted, "Mrs. Burns, do not wait up—we will be back very late." He threw the stair door open, and it banged on the hallway wall. The hallway was dark, and it took a moment for Pettigrew's vision to adjust. He saw Flinders's eager face. *He senses an adventure.*

"What do you think?" said Flinders.

"I think that there is more to this than we know."

"Obviously. But it is an adventure."

"I think so," Pettigrew agreed.

"Then why are we standing here?"

They fairly skipped down the flat's stairs. Pettigrew opened the door. Yellow light and rain flooded through the door frame. Flinders's tall figure was etched in raindrops and lamplight.

He moves like a hound that has been unleashed.

"You wanted some action. Well, now we are going to have it. This case may be bigger than Cleopatra. It will require some serious work on our part."

"Yes," Flinders replied as he stepped out. "But we will not be giving up any fees on this one."

"Are you sure?" Pettigrew asked. "Budge has quite a reputation for not paying his bills."

"Well, we will hold him to it."

"That may be difficult."

"We are done with the six pence; now we look at the moon."

They charged out the door into the drizzle and hailed a cab. Their overcoats smelled of wet wool. Flinders smiled. "As a famous man once said, 'The game is afoot.'" He called out, "Driver, take us to the museum. Drive as fast as you can." He turned. "Once more into the breach, my friend."

Yes, once more into the breach, thought Pettigrew, *and it feels like old times.* He sat back in the seat and smiled to himself. *The hounds have been loosed, Mr. Holmes.*

The cab darted through the wet streets. Its window wipers beat like muffled drums.

The unknown awaited them.

THREE

Once More into the Breach

The museum stood deserted; its shape was shrouded in mist. The Greek horses pranced on its lintel; their shadows shifted as Pettigrew strode under them. Budge and Flinders walked silently at his side. The lamps which lit the grand marble entrance were dark. Gargoyles crouched as black shadows; water trickled off their grinning faces. Light rain splashed off the Ionian columns that guarded the entrance, and a late-night pigeon pecked at the marble steps.

Budge led Flinders and Pettigrew to a small door at the rear of the museum. He unlocked it with a brass key; they entered and followed Budge closely.

"The only people here are the watchmen," Budge explained. "Everybody else left yesterday." The light from Budge's lantern bounced off the marble floors and cast moving shadows of silent statues. They walked among a heaving sea of black-and-white shapes. With a start, Pettigrew realized he had been holding his breath.

As they hurried through the Egyptian and Assyrian galleries, strange faces watched them, faces from another time. Flinders looked around, and Pettigrew could see the glow of fondness and nostalgia etched on his face.

"During the summers when we were away from Oxford, I would come here with my lunch and spend the day," Flinders said. "Imagine sharing a sandwich with Ashurbanipal." He paused in mid-stride. "I felt truly at home here. Perhaps I should have continued as a junior curator." The faces smiled in approval.

Pettigrew nodded. There were memories for him here as well. "There is a medical college a few blocks away," he stated. "I would take classes in the summer. Sometimes I would come here after class and sit in the central court and watch the marble lions."

They passed under the great rotunda. Pettigrew looked up at the stained-glass windows two stories above.

Such beauty. How many times have I looked up at it?

The windows looked down upon him, magnificent, yet stoic. Mythological and medieval figures were portrayed; saints in robes and knights in armor paraded across the heights. Their outlines were dark in the night. But Pettigrew remembered how the morning light would shine through, and the figures would move as the sun moved. Mirror images would slowly cross the marble floor as the hours changed.

What is it about these windows that connects me with my past? I have a sense that I may see these figures again. But in a different way. There is something here, a hint of foreboding, but I cannot put my finger on it.

Budge crossed a narrow hallway and opened another door. Pettigrew saw a winding iron staircase leading up into the dark. Budge pushed ahead, telling them, "This takes us to the Elgin Collection on the second floor. Employees use it. Follow me."

Pettigrew stepped out of the doorway and looked down a brightly lit hall. Pillars supporting the hallway towered three stories in the air, and down the hallway's center was a line of gleaming white marble statues. Tall glass cases filled with artifacts bloomed like icy flowers between the pillars. Pettigrew stared.

"Strange . . . Mike should be up here," Budge said, looking around anxiously. "But I do not see him. He usually comes to me to get petted." Budge grinned in embarrassment. "I cuddle him every day."

Well, that is a surprise, thought Pettigrew. *A soft side to this cold, gruff man.*

At the far end, Pettigrew could see a carved frieze stretching across the wall. "Ah, the horsemen of the Parthenon, the famous Elgin marbles," Flinders noted.

"They have ridden for thousands of years," Pettigrew said quietly. He stared at the scene. Men and horses thunder forward to the Battle of Marathon. Horses rear and paw the air; riders sit proud on their steeds. The white marble comes alive with the drum of hooves and the shouts of men. "They ride as I watch."

What manner of men created these images? Such beauty; such perfection. Who could do this now? Or does anyone care?

"The case is right over here." Budge pointed to a case that stood half-way down the hall. Even from a distance, Pettigrew could see that its glass had been shattered.

"You are quite sure that nobody has been here since the theft?" Pettigrew asked again.

"No one has been here except myself, and I did not go near the case," Budge replied. "Remember, I started out here as the 'store detective' before I became director, so I made sure nothing was disturbed."

"Well done," Pettigrew said.

"It is quite important to the case," Flinders said. "In most of our cases, the crime scene has been completely destroyed." He laughed. "You have no idea of the trouble that creates."

"I do indeed," Budge said with a smile. "I once had a case where some-one walked off with an Assyrian bull. Imagine, it weighed a thousand stone. But the staff had completely cleaned the gallery. There was nothing to go on. We never got it back."

Pettigrew examined the broken glass; he put an arm up against the case. "Flinders," he said, "look at the way this glass has been broken. It's from left to right according to the glass shards. The thief was left-handed. He used his right arm and elbow to steady the glass while breaking it with a muffled instrument, probably a hammer, held in his left hand." Pettigrew pointed. "The pattern of the break suggests that the blow was about chest high—this was done by a short person."

"I see," said Flinders, and he stepped closer to examine it for himself. "From left to right. I think you have it exactly right for once."

Pettigrew pulled something off the broken glass. "There is a piece of cloth on one of the edges. The thief must have been working quickly, and it appears he caught a snag." He peered at it. "I didn't bring my glass, but my guess is that it is a plaid pattern."

"Plaid, is it?" Flinders took the piece of material; his brow furrowed with concentration. He shook his head. "How do you know that this is plaid? Next you will be telling me that it was worn by a bald Royal Marine sergeant who was left-handed, who had a tattoo on his chest, walked with a limp, and was just back from the Khyber Pass."

"I would do no such thing." Pettigrew laughed. "You have me confused with Holmes."

Flinders twirled the threads. "Fortunately, I did bring my magnifying glass. Let us have a look." He held the material and the glass to the light. "Yes. It is houndstooth. Now that makes sense. Why would anyone planning to walk into a museum gallery and steal an artifact wear a plaid coat and thereby risk calling attention to themselves?"

"Flinders, at last you begin to learn. You are correct—houndstooth would be the logical choice." Pettigrew took the material back and pinched it between two fingers. "This is cheap material. The thief was not a rich man." Then he smiled. "But tell me, where did you find that magnifying glass? It looks like one of my old glasses."

"It was in a drawer."

"A drawer, you say."

"In the dining room."

"Yes, that seems to be where I keep mine. I suppose it is fortuitous that you went searching through my things. Perhaps there is something I can help you find." Pettigrew turned and looked at the floor. "There is a trail of glass that leads away from the case." He knelt and began crawling along the floor. "Lend me the glass," he told Flinders.

Flinders handed over the glass and then crouched over and followed him.

"See these?" Pettigrew pointed with a forefinger. "Footprints outlined by glass. You can barely see them."

"I see them," Flinders replied. "The stride between them is short. You were right; the thief was a small man, or perhaps even a woman."

"But the prints have ridges." Pettigrew looked up. "European shoes do not have ridges like these. And there is no toe. We are dealing with someone from outside of Europe. My guess is that the shoes are either Persian or Syrian." He stood up. "I think that we are about done here, but let me have one last look." He put his face close to the sides of the cabinet and sniffed. "There is a strange smell where the glass was broken. Flinders, what do you make of it?"

Flinders sniffed also. "It smells rank, like some sort of tobacco. But certainly not like anything that I have ever smoked." Flinders gestured to Budge. "Director Budge, see what you think."

Budge bent his heavy frame to the spot Pettigrew indicated. He took a deep breath; his glasses fell to the floor. He sniffed and looked up. "Definitely a kind of tobacco, but with a very pungent odor. I smoke cigars regularly, but this is not like any of them. I think that it is foreign, like your footprints."

Flinders nodded. "Very pungent, indeed. But I am not sure it is tobacco."

"Speaking of cigars," Budge said, turning to Flinders, "your uncle and I—before the breakup of course—used to smoke cigars in the Egyptian gallery while we pried open boxes of artifacts." Budge smiled briefly. "Ah, those were the days. The cigar smoke curled around us, and we shouted and laughed as we examined the artifacts." Budge laughed. "The floor would be littered with incredible finds." Budge looked wistful. "Once in a while the find was so magnificent that your uncle would start dancing a jig. The staff would come in to see what all the commotion was about." His eyes clouded with memory. "Your uncle was a connoisseur of cigars. Did you know that he had a collection of cigar bands from all over the world? If he were here, he could tell us exactly where that tobacco came from." Budge looked at the floor. "Sometimes, I miss him."

Flinders smiled and nodded and shot a glance at Pettigrew. "Thomas, can you tell what distinguishing marks the thief had? Scars, tattoos, that sort of thing?"

Budge's eyes widened. "That would be astonishing if he could. Even Holmes could not pull something like that off."

Pettigrew's eyes twinkled as he answered Flinders. "Yes, of course I can. I have an idea what the tattoos looked like, but I think that we need more evidence, just to make sure. Now we must interview the staff." He turned.

"Director Budge, if you would be so kind as to assemble your cleaning crew—and I think we should also talk to your entrance lobby people as well."

An hour or so later, Budge had assembled the cleaning crew and the lobby personnel: six people in drab, gray museum uniforms. They sat on a line of chairs and fidgeted. Some nodded off and then jerked awake, some yawned, and others looked dazed. They sat in a workroom where exhibits were prepared. Stone heads of all sizes, like random bowling balls, littered the floor. Unfinished exhibits lurked in the corners. Dusty glass cases with open doors and misaligned shelves stood like sentries.

Flinders gave the staff a gracious wave. "Please make yourselves comfortable," he told them. "I know we have all had a long day. But I need your help."

Flinders pulled up a chair and crossed his knees. He carefully stretched his trouser crease at the knee and opened a notebook. "Let me see." He brushed his hair back with one hand. He studied the notebook for a moment and then looked up.

"Now, let me count—there should be six of you. One, two, three . . . yes, everybody is here." He smiled. "So, where to begin . . ."

The staff, Pettigrew thought, *looks very unhappy to be here.*

Flinders smiled again and mopped his brow. "It's hot in here, isn't it?" The staff laughed and visibly relaxed. He said in a soft Irish brogue, "A long day indeed. I will be as quick as possible and send you home without wasting any time. To begin, does anyone here know of someone who might have seen a short man in a houndstooth coat?" He looked expectant. "Yesterday, perhaps?"

Budge whispered to Pettigrew, "What is he doing? Why doesn't he ask directly, 'Who saw the man?'"

"Because," Pettigrew patiently explained, "a direct question like that would intimidate a reluctant witness. Accusatory interrogation is what the Metropolitan Police do. It is rather out of date, like truncheons and bright lights."

"I used to do that," Budge said with a grin. "I had a very large leather truncheon."

And no doubt you used it with gusto.

"We all did, once. But no longer. It is far less effective."

"I see." Budge was thoughtful. "The times are changing."

For all of us.

"Pay attention, and you will see something."

Budge nodded.

"Mr. Petrie is a master at what we call 'friendly questioning.' We worked it out with the help of a Viennese physician, a man by the name of Doctor Freud. Marvelous fellow—he was studying what he called the subconscious mind. After the Cleopatra case, we consulted him on dreams and other things."

"Friendly questioning?"

"Yes. It is designed to make the answerer relax and thereby tell the truth. Please be silent and watch. I think you will be pleasantly surprised."

Flinders smiled and looked expectantly at the group, his face pleasant and patient. They shuffled and looked down. Chairs squeaked. Exhibits threw long shadows across the quiet room. After a moment, one of the ladies from the cleaning crew got up and stepped forward. She was very slim and wore a gray dress and carried a brown hat. The hat had a long purple feather. She was hesitant and twisted the hat in her hands; their veins stood out. She stared at the ceiling and stuttered, "My name is Eunice. I thought I saw someone like that. He was walking around outside the Elgin gallery. I didn't notice him at first. But then I saw him; he was just outside the door that leads into the gallery. He must have been walking softly."

The ridged shoes, thought Pettigrew.

"Ah, Eunice, thank you for that," Flinders replied in a conversational tone. "How good of you to come forward." He leaned forward and looked at her. "But do sit down." His eyes were friendly. "You have helped considerably with just those details alone. But could you add a little more? Do you recall anything else?"

"Well," Eunice continued, "he passed by me as he went in the door. He moved strangely—like a cat. He was wearing a coat. I think that it was gray—just like our uniforms. But he smelled terrible. I held my nose. He went right into the Elgin gallery. We had just cleaned it."

She sat back down. The feather quivered. Her chair creaked; its legs scratched on the floor. The cleaning crew behind her rustled uneasily.

"Eunice, you have been most helpful. That was marvelous."

"You see," Pettigrew whispered to Budge. "He's not half bad at this."

Flinders wrote something in the notebook. "Eunice, if you could give me an idea of what he looked like, that would be most helpful. Was he tall or short?"

"He was unusually short."

"What color was his hair?"

"Dark, very dark."

"Long or short? Straight or curly?"

Eunice put her hat down on her lap and frowned. She looked stressed, as if she was trying to remember something. The feather in her hat looked stressed as well. Pettigrew wondered if she was feigning or just tired and confused.

"Long and curly."

Flinders wrote again. He put the pen aside and smiled. Eunice twisted her hat; the feather rippled uneasily. The cleaning crew muttered among themselves. The marble heads were noncommittal. Flinders gave Eunice a little bit of time before he began again.

"Did you see his face?"

"Yes. It was thin, and he had a big nose." That she had no trouble remembering.

Flinders nodded. "Now, Eunice, I want you to think about this. Have you got an idea of what he looked like in your mind?"

Eunice squirmed in her chair, fiddled with her hat, and managed a slight smile. The veins in her hands had relaxed and were much less pronounced.

"I think so."

"Good, very good. Now, if you were going to describe him to a friend, what would you say?"

Aha, very advanced psychology.

Pettigrew turned to smile at Budge. "Observe how he draws her out."

Budge said nothing; he listened in silence.

"He was short and thin and had a little beard. . . . He was foreign-looking. His eyes were dark, and he had a mean look to him. He moved quickly. I was afraid of him. I don't know why—it's not something that happens often to me with strangers. But there was something about him that frightened me." Eunice frowned.

"That is wonderful!" Flinders clapped his hands. "Eunice, you have been a great help."

Eunice's face lit up, and she stood up and managed a brief curtsy before sitting back down.

Pettigrew turned to Budge. "You see how he gets her to relax."

Flinders nodded and smiled. "But did you see anything else?" He sat back and looked thoughtful. "Let me help." He covered his eyes briefly. "Close your eyes for a moment and try to imagine what you would see if you were on the other side of the man. What would you have seen?"

Budge *was* impressed. Pettigrew could see it in his eyes.

Eunice closed her eyes and then stated, "Yes. I saw him come out. I remember that he had a tattoo on his neck. It looked like snakes—like something doctors use to show that it's medicine they practice."

"You mean a caduceus, the symbol of intertwined snakes."

Pettigrew leaned forward in his chair. *Curious. Someone with a tattoo of intertwined snakes steals the statue of a woman entwined by a serpent.*

"Yes, that was it. And he was carrying something. I saw a bulge under his coat."

"Eunice, you have been very brave." Flinders smiled again. "And you have an impressive memory. We could use someone like you in our firm." He clasped his hands together and looked thoughtful. "One more question: Did you see where he was going?"

"Yes, he went down the back stairs." Eunice sat down and breathed a long sigh. She put her hat on and straightened it. The feather drooped in relief.

Flinders asked the group, "Is there anyone else that can contribute anything?" He waited a moment. "No? No one?" He closed the notebook and stood up. "So, that is all for the time being. Thank you. If we need more, Director Budge will contact you."

"Wait." A young man with thinning hair and very large glasses stood up. "My name is Harley. I work at the entrance desk, and I may have seen the man Eunice described." The young man rubbed his balding head and looked pleased with himself.

Another witness. That is good.

Flinders sat down again and reopened his notebook. "Thank you. That is most interesting. What did you see?"

Pettigrew leaned forward to hear.

"I saw a man in a houndstooth coat come through the entrance several times—the entrance desk has been my only post this week, so I saw everyone who came in and out. I noticed him because he kept looking around. Sort of furtive-like, if you know what I mean." The young man turned his head from side to side as a demonstration. The lamplight reflected off his head.

"Yes, I do. And you were very observant in noting this. Did you see anything else?"

"No. The last time I saw him come in was two days ago."

The cleaning crew shuffled. Their chairs rocked. The stone heads watched.

"Curious." Pettigrew scratched an ear. "Eunice said that she saw him pass by yesterday, but the last time he came in the entrance was the day before."

"Director Budge," Flinders said, "are there any side entrances he could have used?"

"No. Only the front entrance. Every other entrance is locked."

"Then we should look for a hiding place somewhere in the building." Pettigrew thought a moment. "It would be a place from where he could observe the gallery."

"There are several broom closets across from the gallery," Budge replied, "but they are all kept locked."

"Nevertheless, we must examine them. No stone unturned."

Budge nodded.

"Anyone else? No?" Flinders checked his notes and then looked up at his audience of six. The six smiled hopefully. "All right, you may all go now. And thank you all for your help."

The staff rose to leave and were shuffling toward the door in a weary line when a man in overalls at the back of the group said, "I think that old George may have seen something. He was in the gallery at the same time Eunice was there. But old George is not here, and I haven't seen him since yesterday." The man pulled on his suspenders. "It's strange, because he is here every day, rain or shine."

The staff nodded.

Flinders stood up. "Wait. Please sit back down for a moment."

The cleaning crew went back to their chairs with a collective sigh. Purses and coats tumbled to the floor. The exhibits listened in hushed silence. The glass case doors opened wider, the better to hear.

"Old George, you say?"

Flinders had stopped looking at his notes; his eyes were suddenly intent. "And he has gone missing?"

"Yes."

"Go on."

"Yes," someone else chimed in. "No one has seen him. He always used to come around in the morning, in time for the coffee we put out for visitors and staff. Old George always had a cup of coffee, and then he would go to the director's office. But he didn't come today."

Budge jumped in. "That's true. I didn't see him this morning. I was too busy with the theft."

"Who is old George?" Pettigrew asked Budge.

"Old George is our oldest curator. He has been around for a thousand years. He noses all over the museum. If there was anything amiss, he would know about it. He is a curating bloodhound." Budge stopped to scowl at Flinders. "Not at all like that terrible fellow your uncle sent me. That man who claimed he could smell fakes."

"Does anyone else know anything about old George? Speak up, please."

The room was still. A woman tapped her heel on the floor; the tapping sounded like canon shots in the silence.

"No? Nothing? Then you may go, truly this time." Flinders smiled and closed his notebook. He looked at Pettigrew.

"So now we have to find old George," Pettigrew said. "Where are these back stairs? I suspect foul play."

"Yes, follow me," Budge said. He took them out of the room and led them through another door and down a flight of iron stairs. "These are only used by the cleaning crew—most employees don't even know that they are here."

They quickly descended. The stair treads were rusted, and the banister shook. Gas lamps flickered an uncertain light. Green paint peeled off the walls, and the gray stair posts were spotted with rust. The stairs creaked and thumped under their feet. When they reached the bottom, they saw a body crumpled along the wall. It had white hair, a short beard, and a green smock. The smock matched the color of the wall. Blood pooled on the floor, and there were spatters on the steps and wall.

Budge peered, put his hands to his face, and then exclaimed, "It is old George! Someone has killed him." He stared at the body. He put his hand on the wall to steady himself and pulled it back when he saw blood on his fingers. Then softly he said, "Old George and I would tour the museum every morning. He knew where everything belonged. After we finished, we would return to my office. I would pour a glass of claret and we would toast the museum." He looked at the ceiling. "Sometimes, when everything was in place, we would have several glasses."

"You were very close?" Flinders said gently.

Budge nodded; his eyes were full of pain. "Old George used to hold his glass up to the light and say, 'It has good color.'" He bent and touched the body. Pettigrew heard him whisper, "My friend, my friend, what have they done to you?"

They let him have a moment.

Eventually, Budge stood up. "The museum was our temple, and we were its guardians." His mouth quivered and his voice shook when he whispered, "Old George was a great friend. The horsemen of the Parthenon were his favorites. He would talk to them. He once told me, 'I think that they hear me across the centuries. Wallis, some nights I come here alone. The riders rein in their steeds and look at me. You cannot imagine.'" Budge steadied himself on the railing. "But I *can* imagine. And now I will drink claret alone and imagine for him." He pulled out a large handkerchief and blew his nose. Tears glistened on his cheek and ran into his mustache.

Pettigrew watched and thought. He wondered if he had ever seen old George, who would have been there at the museum when he was a student. Once he did see an old man in a gray uniform sitting on the marble bench in front of the horsemen.

I paid no attention. But I walked down that gallery and heard their cries. I sat on that bench and felt their terrible energy. Old George and I were really the same. The horsemen called to both of us.

Flinders asked, "Thomas, can you tell anything from the body?"

Pettigrew knelt and examined the body. "He has been stabbed several times, and there are also large slashes on his arms and hands. He clearly put up a fight, but it looks as though he was quickly overpowered."

"You think so," Budge wiped a tear. "Old George would never have given up without a fight."

"A professional assailant?" Flinders asked.

"Probably. The last cut was quite precise."

Pettigrew looked more closely. "The body is cold and quite stiff—rigor mortis has set in. But the stomach gases have not yet expanded. He died sometime late yesterday." Pettigrew turned the body from side to side. "The stab wounds are not that deep. He was killed when his throat was slashed. By the slash marks, I would say that the blade was curved. Yes, the murder weapon was short and curved. Possibly a dagger."

"He fought for his life."

"Indeed so."

"What a shame."

Pettigrew sniffed the body. "It has a strange smell. The same smell as the case upstairs. Flinders, what do you make of this?"

"A curved dagger, a strange smell, and someone with a caduceus tattoo who wears odd shoes. Someone foreign-looking who looks mean, moves quickly, and uses a curved knife. Do I have that right?"

"Indeed, you do."

Flinders thought a moment. "We are dealing with Hashshashin."

"Hashshashin?"

"Yes, the legendary assassins from medieval Syria."

"Are you telling me that a fanatic from the tenth century did this?"

"Yes," Flinders said. "A follower of the Old Man of the Mountain himself."

"Old Man of the Mountain?" Budge echoed.

"Yes, the Grand Master of the Order. He terrified the Islamic world from his mountaintop in Aleppo. No one was safe from his assassins. They even attempted to kill King Richard."

"But we are not in the tenth century and certainly not in Syria," Pettigrew growled. "This is modern London. You speak of ghosts from the past."

"I see what I see." Flinders resolutely crossed his arms. He stared down at the body. "Old George was murdered by an assassin."

"That is not possible. The Hashshashin were destroyed by Hulagu in the thirteenth century. And good riddance, too. I do know a little history—you have got this one wrong, my friend."

"I do not think so," Flinders replied. "The Hashshashin had been in business since the tenth century, and they were not beginners in the art of surviving. We know only that Hulagu destroyed their major fortifications. We do not know how many Hashshashin escaped or what happened to their descendants."

"That is conjecture."

"Maybe so," Flinders added. "What I do know is that whoever murdered old George used a dagger and smelled bad. That smell was probably hashish, not tobacco. The murderer had a tattoo. The tattoo was the traditional mark of the order."

"We need more evidence."

"Ancient orders survive. Look what happened to us in Egypt. The followers of Hermes Trismegistus almost killed us." Flinders frowned. "And they dated from the time of the Ptolemies."

You are right—ancient orders do survive, and so do ancient peoples. But in London?

"An oddity."

But Pettigrew remembered. *They came at us with Greek crossbows. The poisoned darts barely missed us. They whistled past our ears. Inji and I dropped to the ground. The limestone was cold; dust covered us. Flinders stood over us like a granite statue. He laughed at the dark. He drew his pistols and fired. The noise was deafening; the flashes lit up the tomb. I thought the walls would come down. The noise stopped. Flinders blew the smoke from his pistol barrels.*

"Some very active oddities," Flinders said. "And what we see here is comparable."

"We still need more."

"Consider the weapon," Flinders added. "You say that it was curved, a dagger. The Hashshashin were trained in the use of such weapons—they did not use poison or swords. They considered the use of such weapons to be cowardly. They believed in killing at close range. They used hashish to give themselves superhuman strength and courage."

"Many murderers use knives."

"Yes, but the totality of the evidence before us indicates a very special murderer."

"I am still unconvinced." Pettigrew shook his head. "We have a problem. This murderer was hired to steal a statue, and the murder only occurred as the result of a chance meeting. This was not a planned assassination."

"Correct, but the method of his murder is unmistakable." Flinders smiled. "Thomas, remember your Holmes. 'Once you have eliminated the impossible, whatever remains must be the truth.'"

"You may be correct."

Pettigrew finished examining the body, stood up, and turned his attention to the rest of the stairwell. "The blood spatters start about halfway up the staircase. Probably old George was coming up as the murderer came down. There was a fight, and then old George was pushed to the landing floor." He traced the wall. "From the blood on the floor and walls, it appears that the end came where the body now rests."

Budge sighed a deep sigh and took a step away from the body. He turned away and straightened up, but there was a deep sadness in his eyes.

"George, I will carry on for you. Rest assured."

Flinders nodded.

"But let us have a look at the rest of the room." Pettigrew carefully walked around the small area. He stopped in front of a steel door. "Where does this lead?"

"To a back alley outside," Budge explained. "The alley goes out to Montague Place. But nobody ever uses it now. Your Uncle Flinders and I used to bring artifacts through it in the old days." Budge managed a wan smile. "Sometimes the carts would jam in the door, and we would spend hours trying to pry them loose. Your uncle would scream and whoop and laugh. Old George would pound on the door frame. I would hand them a flask of brandy. We didn't need glasses." He sighed. "Your uncle is gone. There are no more artifacts. There is no more dancing. Nobody uses that door now."

"Well, somebody did." Pettigrew examined the door. "The murderer went out through it. There are bloody handprints on the jam and the knob." Pettigrew closely inspected the door. "There is a piece of paper stuck in the jam." He carefully pulled it out. "The door is heavy. From the prints, it looks like the murderer had to use both hands to push it open. This paper probably slipped out of his sleeve or pocket."

Pettigrew studied the paper for a long moment. "It has Arabic writing on it." He gingerly handed it to Budge. "I cannot read it, but maybe you can."

"I read several languages. Arabic is one of them." Budge peered at the paper more closely. "It is written in Ottoman Turkish. I taught myself to read Ottoman Turkish." Budge became professorial in tone; the tremble in his voice was gone. "Ottoman Turkish is a composite of Arabic, Persian, and Turkish. It is the language of bureaucrats, and it is designed to conceal meaning." He pulled the rimless spectacles from his pocket and put them on. "But let me see what I can do."

Budge began to read, translating to English as he went.

> *From the Most noble of Men,*
> *His Divine and Merciful Highness,*
> *Lord of the Diwan and all things earthly,*
> *May he be praised of Allah,*

To his most trusted of Servants,
He who is strong in body and Spirit,
He who must be feared in the night,
May he carry out that which has been
Committed and foresworn,
And earn everlasting Glory.

Budge stopped reading. "There is no signature."

A strange message, Pettigrew thought.

"Can you say anything about the writer?"

"A little." Budge scrutinized the paper. "I am trained in interpreting scripts." He twisted the paper in his hands and bent over it. "The lettering and phrasing would indicate that the note comes from an important official." He looked up. "More, I cannot tell."

Flinders took the note and examined it with the magnifying glass. "The paper is odd. There is a vellum-like sheen to it, and it is interspersed with gold threads. It reminds me of some medieval manuscripts I studied at Oxford." Flinders turned the paper over. "There is writing on the back. It is in a different script." He held the paper out. "Director Budge, can you decipher it?"

Budge took the paper again. He squinted through his spectacles. He shook his head. "I can barely make this out. It is in Arabic. Give me a moment to study it." He turned the paper sideways to get a better view. Finally, he spoke. "The ink is blurred, but I think it says, 'Deliver the possessed to He who commands at the Qal'at al-Hisn on the eleventh day after the moon rises. When the prayer and fasting end. When a black thread cannot be distinguished from a white thread.'"

Budge continued, "Qal'at al-Hisn is the Arabic name for the Krak des Chevaliers, the most famous crusader castle in Syria. If I am correct, your murderer is to deliver the statue to someone at the Krak in the evening on the last day of Ramadan." Budge handed the paper to Flinders. "Ramadan will begin next week."

"Curious," Pettigrew muttered. "The strange part of all this is why would someone hire an assassin to rob a museum? If, in fact, one could hire an assassin at all?" He rubbed his chin. "So we are up against a blank wall. We know the general identity of the thief and murderer. We know that someone sent him. We know where the statue is to be delivered." He looked at Flinders. "But to whom it was to be taken and where the statue is right now remains a mystery."

"True."

"There remains one more question." Pettigrew frowned. "From what the witnesses said, the murderer was in the building for the duration of at least one night. Before we go further, we must find the murderer's hiding place."

The three climbed the iron staircase and entered the gallery. The gallery was empty; the lamps had been turned down. Its tall windows were dark, and raindrops ran down them. Fitful shadows chased one another across the marble floor. White busts floated in the gloom. The horsemen paused mid-gallop. They walked; their footsteps rang hollow in the silence.

"There are three closets on this floor. The gallery is visible from all three. But they are locked."

They walked down the hall. Pettigrew tried each door as they passed. "This one is not. The lock has been broken." Pettigrew carefully opened the door. Its hinges squeaked.

They looked in. They jumped back in horror at what they saw. Pettigrew stared and then drew back. A gray cat lay on the floor. Its yellow eyes were wide and sightless. Its head had been twisted around until its neck was broken.

"My God! That is Mike. The monster has killed Mike." Budge's face turned red. "He has killed my friend!" Budge sunk to his knees. He steadied himself by holding the door jam. "What beast kills an old man and then an old gray cat for no reason?" His voice rose. "Why kill them? I am here." He reached out to stroke the cat and then stood up. "Face me first, you coward." He shook his clenched fists. "Face me. Face me!"

His cry echoed down the long hall and reverberated off the still exhibits. The horsemen of the Parthenon reined in their steeds and listened. Marble faces turned. The museum held its breath.

"This is too much. First George, now Mike." He knelt and whispered again, "This is too much. First George, now Mike."

Flinders reached down and helped him up. Pettigrew gingerly lifted

Mike's body. It was stiff and cold. He handed it to Budge. Budge folded it in his arms and caressed the cat's head. Tears streamed down his cheeks. He rocked the cat back and forth and crooned. The dim light caught the tears. The silken Saville Row was stained.

Flinders and Pettigrew turned away.

First old George and now Mike. He has no one.

The light from the lamps shone on an old man hugging an old cat—a solitary figure who swayed and grieved, a dark and sorrowful form in the midst of serene splendor.

Pettigrew looked at Flinders. "What now?"

"We must continue," said Flinders.

Pettigrew and Flinders combed through the closet. It was filled with brooms and towels. A dirty blanket was spread on its floor.

"Aha," Flinders said. "I rest my case. The Hashshashin watched their intended victims for days or weeks, and so did this one." Flinders pointed to some empty food wrappers. "Look, there are even unopened food items in this corner—he clearly intended to spend days here, if necessary." He rummaged through the towels. "There is something else." Flinders held up an old newspaper. "From the looks of this, it must be almost fifty years old." He handed it to Budge, saying, "It looks like Arabic. Can you read it?"

"It is in Ottoman Turkish."

Budge wiped the tears from his face and read. "It describes the execution of a traitor and his family and the seizure of their property."

"Curious that an assassin would have such a thing," said Pettigrew.

"Director Budge," Flinders said, "did you ever inquire as to why the general sold his statue?"

"I did, but all he would say was that it was cursed." Budge reflected. "But every artifact in this museum is cursed in some way or another." He managed a wan smile. "Perhaps I should put an exorcist on staff."

"There is more." Flinders held up a scarf.

Budge examined it. "It is a *kufiyah*, a headscarf."

Flinders examined the scarf. "Odd that he should leave it behind. A staff member probably opened the closet door, and he fled. From the design, I would say that it is Syrian."

"Syrian?" said Pettigrew, and he took the scarf. "It is new."

"So now we have a Syrian connection." Flinders was thoughtful. "A missing artifact, a murder, and a curse. Clearly, we need some expertise in the provenance of these things." He looked at Pettigrew intently. "Thomas, your father is in the artifact business. He deals with these people all the time. If anyone could provide us with information about the person who ordered this theft, he could."

"Yes, that would be a start."

Budge nodded. "I use Thomas Senior all the time to help authenticate artifacts. He is most knowledgeable." He added, "And if he cannot, I know several antiquarians who study these manuscripts."

"I think that you are right," Pettigrew agreed, though he wondered what his father would say. He hadn't seen him in years.

I left home years ago. My father wanted me to carry on the family business. I wanted to be a detective. Now, I come back and ask for his help.

The detectives prepared to go, and the three of them made their way outside. They descended the marble steps. Rain beat down on their umbrellas. Budge staggered in the wet, and Flinders steadied him as he hailed a cab. Pettigrew opened the cab door; rain fell on the seats. Pettigrew turned to Budge. "Goodbye for now, Director Budge. We may be out of touch for a while. You had better call the police to take care of the body. We must move at once."

"Of course," said Budge. "There is no time to waste. The end of Ramadan approaches."

The cab door swung open wider. Flinders and Pettigrew closed their umbrellas. Budge stood on the curb as rain streamed off his umbrella. His hair was wet, and his overcoat was soaked. Pettigrew paused before getting in and touched Budge's shoulder. "And Director, do not worry—we will bring your Aphrodite back."

Budge nodded. His eyes were swollen.

As the cab pulled away, Pettigrew looked back at the museum. The forlorn figure of Director Budge waved goodbye. Sheets of rain swirled around the marble pillars. The museum's outline was etched by a pale aura. Yellow light from the streetlamps bathed its steps. The museum receded and grew smaller and finally disappeared.

They rode in silence for a time. Then Pettigrew turned and said, "I told him we would recover his statue. I do not usually make such promises."

Flinders nodded. "It is now a matter of honor."

"Yes, a matter of honor."

FOUR

The Sailor Returns

"Hello there!" Thomas Pettigrew Senior said. "Thomas, you have come back, and Flinders too." He opened the large front door. Slightly balding, with a clean chin and laugh wrinkles, Pettigrew Senior had the same periwinkle blue eyes as his son. He held a slender-stemmed meerschaum pipe.

He still smokes the same old pipe. I remember the smell of his tobacco.

"Tommy boy," he proclaimed, hugging his son, "it's so good to see you. Flinders, you haven't aged a bit. Do come in out of the rain and make yourselves comfortable." He pushed them through the door. "The house is in disorder—we are setting up for an unwrapping tonight, and we expect more than three hundred people. Put your slickers over there."

I come home after all these years, and I feel like a sailor whose ship has returned to port and sees his family again after years at sea. I am the Flying Dutchman, allowed one short visit on land.

"'Tommy boy,' is it?" Flinders grinned at Pettigrew.

Pettigrew winced; his face flushed. "Never mind that."

My father still laughs the same laugh. But he is aging and now walks with a cane.

Pettigrew Senior led the two through a labyrinth of halls and rooms—Pettigrew had always thought that the house was much larger than it appeared from the outside.

When I was small, everything here looked huge.

"You have no idea of just how much work it is to put one of these showings on," Pettigrew Senior burbled as they walked. "Tommy, I must show you everything. It's been so long, so very long."

As they passed a large portrait, Pettigrew stopped and pointed it out to Flinders. "That is my grandfather, Thomas Pettigrew. He was a famous anatomist and popularized mummy openings—people called him 'Mummy Pettigrew.' My father has his name and nickname, and so do I." Pettigrew winced; his face flushed. "Remember when our fellow students used to call me 'mummy's boy'?"

"Ah, yes, I remember them shouting and laughing." Flinders grinned. "We should have pommeled them."

"I'm sorry for that." Pettigrew Senior had overheard. "They called my father that, and then me, and finally you. When my father practiced at Charing Cross Hospital, the nurses made up a rhyme about mummies. They used to sing it when he passed by. My father hated it. That is the price we pay for what we do. But if we advance the study of anatomy, so be it." He laughed. "Blame it on your ancestors. So, my son, what is it that brings you here?"

The cane tapped on the floor as he walked. Pettigrew studied his father. He was balder now; the dark hair he remembered had given way to gray. The once slim figure was heavier. But he still wore the same old coat with the wide lapels, and his father's heavy gold watch still hung on its chain.

My father once told me about the watch. Queen Victoria had given it to his father after he vaccinated her. My grandfather was very proud of it. My father said, "My son, one day this watch will be yours."

Pettigrew stopped walking and turned to face him. "Father, we need your help. A statue of Aphrodite has been stolen from the museum. The thief appears to have been a member of the Order of Assassins. There is a firman that says the statue is to be delivered to a crusader castle in Syria."

Pettigrew Senior stopped walking. He put his pipe down. His smile disappeared.

"Assassins, you say? A firman, you say? You have gotten yourselves into very difficult territory." He sat down on a carved marble sphinx, one of many that lined the hallway. "Let me see the firman."

Pettigrew Junior handed it to him, and Pettigrew Senior examined the paper; he looked concerned. "Where did you find this?"

"We found it in the museum," Flinders said. "A man was murdered. This parchment was near his body."

"Murdered?" Pettigrew Senior looked up at his son. Then he nodded. "Yes, I have seen something like this before. You are dealing with a very dangerous man." He stood up. "I will show you around while I think about your statue." He gestured toward the end of the hallway.

As they walked, Pettigrew whispered, "Flinders, I have not been here in years. But nothing seems to have changed. I can hear my mother playing the piano in the parlor. She loved to play Schubert."

Pettigrew stopped and thought, *I would come home from school. I would open the door. I would hear the piano notes echoing down the halls as I entered. The notes would ripple down the hallway like water sparkling in a fountain. Sometimes, when I was very young, I would throw my schoolbooks down and dance to them.*

"Are you all right?" asked Flinders.

"Yes. The feeling is strange—it's as though I am returning to my boyhood."

"Curious," said Flinders. "But it is true that memories can come flooding back, and quite powerfully, if something jogs the mind."

"Curious, indeed."

"Remember what happened in Egypt," Flinders replied. "Inji often described memories of some past life. Memories that could only have come from Cleopatra herself."

"Yes, and afterward we consulted Doctor Freud about those memories."

Memories . . . everything is the same. I am a boy again; I walk along these halls and look at the curtains and portraits. My mother calls out, "Tommy, come to dinner."

"Ahem," his father interrupted. "Business is declining. No one seems to be interested in mummies nowadays." Pettigrew Senior frowned. "But we keep going."

They reached a large auditorium. In front was a long wooden stage. Its boards were scarred from years of use. Rows of seats stretched to the rear of the room. Some attendants were mopping the stage floor, dusting the chairs and arranging them in the rows. Others carried large vases of lilies. A few were bustling about setting up drink and food trays. Still others were adjusting the gas lamps that hung from the ceiling. Heavy black velvet drapes lined the walls. Pettigrew Senior fingered one of the drapes and said, "We replace them every couple of years. Over time they get ratty and look disreputable."

"We used to set up twice a month," Pettigrew told Flinders. "My father would make me arrange the chairs."

The chairs were heavy. Their legs scraped on the floor as I pushed them. The room smelled of lilies, incense, and juniper berries. Sometimes a maid named Doris would help me. She was tall and smelled like roses. She would laugh and say, "Hurry, your father is waiting." I felt very small.

"A string trio sits in this alcove," Pettigrew Senior said, pulling aside a drape and revealing a small alcove. "We write our own music, always something Egyptian-sounding." He pulled at his lapels. "I have a young composer from one of the local music academies on retainer. The music sets the mood beautifully."

Then he frowned. "So, Director Budge wants you to bring his statue back. I am not sure that I want to help you."

"Why, if I may ask, are you unsure?"

"For several reasons . . ." He moved on and led them toward a large door covered with carvings of papyrus plants. "Over here"—Pettigrew Senior pointed toward a small door—"we have a nurse's station. Quite often, people are overcome when I am performing a dissection, so I added nurses. They come over from Saint Bartholomew's."

I often saw them; they dressed in black and wore white caps with little wings.

"Usually people just faint, but we have had a few heart attacks. And there was one old fellow that had a stroke many years ago."

The man was in a back row. My father rushed over and caught him before he could fall off his chair.

"But we haven't had any problems for a few years now." Pettigrew's father smiled. "We try to anticipate everything." He laughed wryly and opened the carved door. "Now, let me show you the preparation room where the mummies are kept."

Pettigrew Senior held the door open, and they entered.

"The man you want is in Istanbul. But you will have to go through Syria to find him." He pushed them through another door at the side of the stage. "Come and see. Tommy, do you remember this?"

The room was bare except for several large gurneys neatly lined up. At one end were three or four wooden sarcophagi of differing sizes. "We select the sarcophagus to match the mummy. They are made of wood because granite sarcophagi would be too heavy to move." He chuckled and patted one of the elaborate tombs. "We have a cabinetmaker in Cairo who specializes in making sarcophagi. He can conjure up a really clever one, very authentic-looking, in about three weeks." Pettigrew Senior paused again. "The man you are seeking is very dangerous—very dangerous indeed."

Pettigrew listened. *Why is he so reticent to speak? I know my father, and this silence is not like him. Let me see what I can do to get him to talk.* "Father, could you elaborate? Director Budge was certain that you could provide some answers."

"Let us finish the tour and then have dinner. I want to show you everything. You have been away for so long."

He pulled a sarcophagus cover open. "Flinders, come over here and see this. It just came in from Kom Ombo, and it's in very fine condition."

Pettigrew turned to Flinders. "As a boy, I used to help put the mummies in their sarcophagi. Sometimes they would fall apart, and we would have to tape them together. It was painstaking work, and we had to keep the tape hidden from view as much as possible."

Once, a hand fell on the floor. It looked like a large spider ready to pounce. The audience screamed. My father laughed and picked it up.

Pettigrew Senior closed the sarcophagus cover.

"Thomas." He looked at his son. "Are you sure you want to continue your investigation?"

"Father, we traveled to Egypt in search of Cleopatra," Pettigrew said with a laugh. "We were shot at by crossbows, strangled with steel garrotes, and assaulted by villains. And we managed to come back in one piece."

"You do not understand." His father shook his head. Then he led them into a small room. White walls reflected bright lamplight. Iron gurneys lined one side. The room was cold, and there was a faint smell of juniper.

"The mummies are brought in through that door," said Pettigrew Senior. He pointed to a double door. "Then they are placed in a sarcophagus on one of the gurneys. We keep the gurneys' wheels well oiled—in the old days, the wheels used to squeak, and it was distracting." He laughed. "Once, one of the wheels fell off—the cart flipped and dumped the mummy into the first row."

Its head came off, and it landed in some elegant gentleman's lap. He was horrified. He threw it across the room and then promptly fainted. My father called the nurse. Pettigrew remembered the shrieks and screams. *But there is something behind these stories. They are all disasters of sorts. Is he warning me that he fears another disaster?*

"Flinders, you should have been there."

Pettigrew Senior refilled his pipe. "I select the mummy for the night and prepare it for dissection. When I cut into these things, I never know what I will find. Once, I opened a skull, and a snake jumped out at me and started slithering toward the audience. People screamed and started running for the doors. Top hats and ladies' shawls flew all over the place. They even broke a few chairs." He grinned. "Actually, it was rather fun."

My father calmly grabbed the snake with his forceps and put it in a basket.

Pettigrew laughed. "Flinders, the same thing happened once before. My father was on the stage. He was magnificent, standing there and lecturing to the audience. I was so proud, and I remember thinking, *That is my father.* I wanted to be like him. Then a rat jumped out of the mummy's skull and skittered toward him. My father dodged it and continued lecturing as though nothing had happened."

Flinders laughed. "Your father is quite the man."

"Flinders, I can never live up to him."

But now there is a look in his eyes. A worry that I cannot put my finger on.

"Cleopatra, is it?" Pettigrew Senior frowned. "That may be quite true, but are you quite sure you know what you're getting into?" Then he smiled. "It's always a delight when the lights go on, and the audience is assembled. We replaced the old candles with gas lamps, and we are thinking about installing electric lights. The National Gallery has just gone electric, and so have most of the public buildings, and we may follow their lead. But when the music starts, the lights matter little. . . . Our violinist is really quite good." He put a hand on Pettigrew's shoulder. "Please think about what you are about to undertake."

My father banters, but all this happy talk about mummies is not what he really means.

Pettigrew Senior thumped his chest. "Well, enough of that." He pointed to the stage. "We have work to do. The show must go on."

"Flinders, I used to love that part," Pettigrew said. "I would hide in the back behind a curtain where I was sure no one could see me and watch the exhibition. The audience would stare at the mummies; there was awe and wonder on all their faces."

But my father saw me. He came right over to where I was hiding and said, "The show is over—it is time for bed." He always knew where I was. Maybe that is what's behind his eyes now. He won't know where I am. He won't be able to protect me.

Pettigrew Senior continued. "Everyone who is anyone comes to our show—we get boodles of notables. Just about every member of royalty has been here." He smiled with pride. "Once, years ago, the Queen herself attended. She sat in the front row just opposite me. I bowed and invited her to come onstage. Oscar Wilde often sits in the back and smokes—once he said he was getting ideas for a poem about sphinxes." He frowned. "Of course, we discourage smoking. Mummies are very dry, and they burn easily. You cannot imagine how awful a burning mummy smells. One caught fire a year ago, and the stench lasted for weeks." Pettigrew Senior straightened a curtain. "We must be very careful about fire. Fire and smoke can destroy us."

"Fire and smoke?"

Now he talks about fire. I have never heard him talk about fire and smoke before.

"Flinders, I remember when a fire broke out years ago. Smoke covered everything. The audience ran all over the place. Ladies were fainting left and right. One old gentleman had a heart attack. The fire brigade rushed in and started squirting water at everything. My mother grabbed me and pulled me out into the street."

She was very afraid and had held me tight. She looked at the smoke and cried. What is there about fire that threatens us so?

"Come along. We will go back through the auditorium. Right in here."

They followed. The carved door closed behind them; the papyrus plants swayed with its movement.

"The American writer Edgar Allan Poe used to come by when he was in town. He once told me that he got the idea for a short story, 'The Mummy Awakens,' from watching me. He gave me an autographed copy. I keep it in my office. It was about a mummy that suddenly sat up and started to talk. That was years and years ago. Too bad he died so young."

Rows of chairs stretched before them.

"But think about it." He placed a finger alongside his nose and opened his eyes wide like an owl. "What would happen if a mummy sat up, said, 'Hello,' and started unwrapping its bandages? Ladies would swoon; men would faint. Chairs would fly. The fire brigade would be called." He spread his arms. "The horse guards would charge. Sabers would flash; cannons would fire." He spun around. "The mayor and council would tumble in. Church bells would ring." He flourished his pipe. "General Kitchener would issue orders. The prime minister would declare an emergency. The king would look stern and call for calm."

He collapsed onto a chair, exhausted from his own theatrics. "Gilbert and Sullivan would come out of retirement and write one last opera." He convulsed with laughter. "We would be immortalized." He got up, still shaking with laughter. "My son, it feels good to see you again. I haven't laughed in years, not since your mother died." He hugged Pettigrew.

Since your mother died. Pettigrew covered his face with his hands. *I used to play cricket after school. I loved the tick of the ball and the shouts of the players. Late one afternoon, when the sun had just started going down and the field turned cold, my father came. He said, "Your mother has just died." She was in the hospital for days. My father never left her. Then he hugged me, and we both cried. "I will always protect you, like your mother did." He then retired to his room. When I passed by his door, I could hear him crying. The piano was silent.*

"Flinders, when my mother died, my world ended in that moment."

Pettigrew Senior now looked very serious. "Thomas, are you sure that you want to go through with this? Why don't you join me? We had great times together once." Then he softened. "Yes, great times."

If I could only go back to being a boy again . . . but I cannot. I cannot. When I was a boy, the sun was brighter, the flowers smelled sweeter, and the girls were prettier. Now I am a middle-aged man, and the sheen of life is fading.

"But the business is getting tougher. It used to be that we had a regular pipeline to Egypt. All sorts of people would bring us mummies. We would store them in a warehouse." Pettigrew Senior gestured at Flinders. "Your uncle was most helpful in supplying us with contacts. Now, the Egyptian government is cracking down on mummy export—you have no idea how difficult it is to smuggle a mummy. We usually hide them in carcasses of large animals sent to museums for taxidermy and display. You have to wrap them up carefully; even so, their arms and legs tend to fall off."

Mummies. Pettigrew remembered them bringing in the mummies. They were strapped down on large carts. *These were men once. They laughed and cried; they dreamed and fought. Life was as good for them as it is to me. Now, they lie lifeless in large carts. How can we do this to them?*

His father grinned. "It is very bad form to have an arm flop on the floor in front of a customs officer." He chuckled. "That always required some very fast talking."

"Flinders, I miss this so terribly." *But I have another life now. I cannot go back, no matter how much I yearn.*

Flinders nodded. "We have come too far from the days when we were innocent boys."

"Now we are men. Is it worth it?"

"I am not sure." Flinders looked at his boots. "I miss my father; now nothing is safe."

"Now nothing is safe." Pettigrew turned to his father. "As I remember, I stood beside you and watched you bamboozle one when he came to the house."

He was magnificent. He stood there with his arms akimbo and said, "What arm? I didn't see any arm. That was a tree branch that got caught on the container. Let me shake your hand." They shook hands, and the officer turned and left. "Goodbye, sir." My father looked down at me. "My son," he said, "sometimes we must do what we must do." I did not know what he meant. Then he laughed and said, "I'm hungry. How 'bout you?"

"Indeed. I had forgotten that. You stood beside me, and your eyes were big as doorknobs." His father laughed and tapped tobacco into his pipe. "But you didn't come here to talk about mummies. I can see that you are determined to go on. All right, I will try and help. What can I do for you?" Pettigrew Senior waved them into the dining room. "Come, sit down and tell me everything you know. Of course, you will stay for dinner and then see the show." He gave Pettigrew a fatherly smile. "We will be able to say, 'There is a doctor in the house.'"

"Flinders, this is so familiar."

How many times have I eaten dinner in this room? The old table is the same; the chandelier is the same. The purple walls are the same.

"Flinders, nothing has changed. I remember when my mother and father debated what color to paint the walls—my mother wanted purple; my father wanted dark green. They argued for days. Finally, my father threw his arms up in the air and said, 'Purple it is.' They hugged for a very long time. Flinders, I miss her."

"You never spoke of her."

"No, I never did. The memory is too painful."

"I lost my mother as well. She would always scrub my face and comb my hair and say, 'Flinders, you are a gentleman. Gentlemen are always elegant. Gentlemen are always courteous.' I have tried to follow her advice."

"Then she died."

"And now what are we?"

"I do not know."

"Come on," Pettigrew Senior called out. "It's time for dinner, and I'm hungry."

After dinner, they sat at the cleared table. A maid brought a decanter of brandy. Pettigrew Senior opened a box of cigars. Gas lamps flickered; crystal sparkled. The room still smelled of roast beef and cabbage. Cigar smoke circled their heads. Pettigrew Senior told stories about his own youth.

"My father introduced me to your uncle and Wallis Budge. They were just starting out. My father made connections for them. When I was a young man, he used to send me to Egypt with them. We would open sites and collect mummies. Then, after weeks in the desert, we would go to the Mena House and drink brandy. Later, Lord Cromer joined us."

He smiled at Flinders. "Your uncle was very much the man about town then. After a few drinks, he would go off to see the ladies. He was very fond of one of them. I think her name was Agatha. She was very young and came to Egypt every year with her parents." He laughed. "Budge would just sit there. I think he was very jealous. But enough of that." He picked up the crumpled paper. "There are dark stains on it." He looked at his son. "Blood?"

Pettigrew nodded.

Pettigrew Senior studied the paper and frowned. "As I said, I have seen these before." He stared into his glass. "The first time was when I was a surgeon aboard HMS *Victory*. We had been ordered to the Black Sea and made port in Istanbul. A man was brought aboard—he was horribly mutilated. Both his hands were cut off. A stake had been driven through one eye; a bloody paper like this one was tied to it. I couldn't save him. The Istanbul police looked on but wouldn't say a word." He thumped his glass on the table.

"After I got ashore, I asked the counsel about it. He said it was an order to kill . . . and refused to say anything else." He poured himself another glass. "When we made port in London, I went to Whitehall and asked about the man. Nobody would say anything. Finally, a young intelligence officer told me that the killing was part of a terrible vengeance that had been going on for decades. He advised me to stay clear." Pettigrew Senior examined his glass and looked thoughtful.

"The second time was many years later." He smiled at Pettigrew. "You were just a boy." He took a sip of brandy. "We had just received a large shipment of mummies. Because of customs, we had to route it through Syria. I opened the first two or three—nothing seemed amiss. The performance went on as usual. But the third . . ." Pettigrew Senior rolled his eyes. "When I opened the third, it wasn't a mummy. It was a dead man wrapped as a mummy."

He took another sip and leaned forward. His eyes widened. "I could not believe my eyes." Pettigrew Senior put his glass down. "I saw something that was once a man but now was a man with his throat cut from ear to ear.

I said to the assistants, 'Bring me another mummy.' I turned to the audience—thank God they couldn't see what I saw—and said, 'This mummy is too damaged to dissect. We need to bring in another. Please bear with me for a few moments.'"

Pettigrew Senior took another drink. "We wheeled in a different mummy and finished the show. I went back to the preparation room. When I looked at the corpse, I saw the same kind of paper pinned to its chest that I saw in Istanbul. It looked exactly like the one you have brought. So I made inquiries."

He swirled the brandy. "My contact in Damascus reported back. She said that the man who writes these orders is known only as the Veiled One. He was once an officer in the Fifth Army and stationed in Baghdad. But he was convicted of brutally murdering two fellow officers and sentenced to death. He escaped his prison cell and fled to the mountains somewhere on the Turkish-Syrian border. His second in command is called the Bulbul Pasha—the 'nightingale' or 'executioner.' He is said to sing softly as he strangles his victims. The sultan has put a bounty on both their heads. Ottoman police have been searching for them for years."

He put his elbows on the table and leaned forward. His eyes were dark.

"The Veiled One is a very evil man. But there is more." He suddenly looked very tired. He folded his napkin, leaned back in his chair, and started to speak, when an assistant opened the carved walnut door and poked his head in.

"Sir, it is time to get ready. We are expecting a large crowd tonight. A member of the royal family has sent word that he will be attending."

"Well, then." Pettigrew Senior folded his napkin. "Our conversation will have to wait." He stuffed out his cigar. "We shall have to get a leg on. Flinders, you will have the honor of bringing the mummy in. Push the cart slowly, and don't smile. You can help with the unwrapping—the first set of bandages goes on the floor. The inside white bands go in the wooden box. Then just stand back and look solemn. Don't trip on the bandages!"

They stood up.

"Son, you can help with the dissection. Stand to my right, and hand me the instruments. I'm going to let you make a cut or two. When I extract the brain, I'll give it to you. Just hold it up so the audience can see it. Walk to the front of the stage. If you see anyone fainting out there, signal the nurse. She'll be in the back to your right. Don't forget the gloves! You know where they are."

He opened the door. "All right, then, let us go!"

Pettigrew Senior hustled the two along the hall and into the preparation room. The mummy was already on the cart. Flinders grabbed the cart's handles. Pettigrew straightened his tie and pulled on his gloves. He could hear the audience filing in.

I haven't heard this sound in years. The excitement moves me. I become young again.

Pettigrew Senior signaled. The stage curtains opened, the gas lights brightened, and out they went onstage into the brightness. The audience was a sea of black figures behind the bright stage lights. Pale faces reflected the light from the stage; smiles lined the rows. Latecomers struggled into their seats. People clapped; violins played. The house was full. Pettigrew Senior strode to the front of the stage.

"Welcome. Welcome. Tonight, we have the honor of presenting you with a real Egyptian mummy, a memorial of ancient antiquity. Together, we shall unveil its secrets." He bowed. "Now, let us begin." He turned. "Bring in the mummy."

The audience clapped.

The cartwheels rolled forward. Flinders pushed it; his strides were measured as though he were carrying a coffin at a funeral. The uneven stage caused the cart to sway back and forth. The mummy shifted in rhythm.

The audience gasped. "It's alive!"

Ladies covered their faces with scarves; men tilted bowlers over their noses. Pettigrew Senior pointed to the front of the stage. Flinders rolled the cart to a stop. The audience leaned forward in their seats.

"Remember these?" Pettigrew smiled at his son as he took saws, knives, and scissors from a worn leather case. He held up a saw. Its blade glinted in the stage lights. The audience squirmed. Pettigrew examined it and ran a finger along the blade. He turned toward the audience and lifted an eyebrow.

The audience shivered.

"And now, let us begin. Flinders, the bandages, please."

The saw made an unpleasant rasping noise. Flakes of bone whirled about and then fell to the floor. Ladies pulled their coats tight across their necks; men "ahemed" and steepled their hands over their noses.

Pettigrew began to hum "Flow Gently, Sweet Afton." Flinders picked up the melody in a smooth baritone; Pettigrew Junior added a heavy bass line. The audience covered their ears.

How many times have I heard that melody? Father, it has been so long. I see a ray of sunshine streaming out from behind a dark cloud.

"Now you take the brain." Pettigrew Senior held out a dark, tarry mass. His eyes were bright. The audience gurgled.

I take it with my forceps. Our eyes meet. His smile pierces my heart.

"Hold it up so the audience can see."

We are father and son again.

The audience shuddered.

After the show was over and the audience had left, Pettigrew helped his father clean up.

"It was a great success tonight," Pettigrew Senior said. "A great success, indeed." He smiled. "I am very pleased; we haven't had this much excitement in years." He looked wistful for a moment. "It was like the old times." He frowned. "But then the old times never come back. The boy I knew has now become a man."

He turned away and studied the preparation room. Then he turned back, laughed, and affectionately clapped Pettigrew on the shoulder. "You were magnificent. When you held that brain out and then appeared to drop it—even though I had told you to look serious!—I thought the audience was going to have a collective conniption. You are a natural showman. And speaking of brains—Tommy, do you remember when a stray cat got in? It ran across the stage, jumped on the mummy, and pawed at the brain as I held it up."

He pushed it away with his free hand. It ran to where I was. I grabbed it and handed it to my mother. My father winked at me.

"Yes, that was fun."

Pettigrew Senior took off his gloves and locked the preparation room door.

"And my performance, sir?" Flinders said teasingly.

"Flinders, you were astonishing." Pettigrew Senior laughed as the trio walked back to the dining room. "You have clearly missed your calling. I thought the mummy was going to sit up when you pushed it onstage." He put an arm around his son. "And, Tommy, you looked like Doctor Frankenstein himself; you put on a horrible grin and waved that scalpel like a true monster." He laughed. "I am blessed with two such able assistants." He pulled Pettigrew tight and whispered, "But I have only one son." Then he pushed him away and peered at him strangely. "My son, you are taller than I am."

I will never be taller than you are.

Pettigrew Senior opened the door and ushered them in. The dining room was empty. The gas lamps glowed softly. The three sat down, and Pettigrew Senior poured the brandy.

"Now, where were we?" He sat in a large chair decorated with Egyptian heads. "I got this in Cairo many years ago—it is my favorite chair."

My father used to sit in that chair and say, "This chair is for the man of the house." My mother would laugh and say, "Are you sure you don't mean for the mouse of the house?"

The table had been cleared except for the decanter and a silver box of cigars embossed with Egyptian figures.

"Do have a cigar while I think." Pettigrew Senior took a cigar and lit it. "Ah yes, the young officer was terribly disfigured during his escape. That is why he wears a veil and is called the Veiled One. The Veiled One is said to be very brutal—he enjoys watching hangings while he eats breakfast. He personally tortures people, even though he could easily have someone do it for him. Sometimes he drives a hot iron through their ears; other times he cuts them apart with a small knife, starting with their fingers. He has had whole villages impaled."

He leaned across the table; his elbows wrinkled the tablecloth. "My son, this is true evil." He reached for the decanter. "As for the Bulbul Pasha, he is said to be a giant of a man. He smashes men's heads together and laughs. My contact said there were stories—stories that say he eats human flesh for dinner. And that he strangles women without number."

Pettigrew Senior poured himself another glass. "But these are only stories, possibly no more than wild rumors." He took a sip. "Yes, only stories like old Arabian legends about jinns."

"Jinns?"

"Yes, jinns, an ancient people who were said to be hideous in appearance. But their deformities mirrored their inner evilness."

Deformities. Like the beggar and the circus freaks. But were their deformities because of their evilness, or because of some evil that happened to them?

Flinders spoke up. "But as you say, they may just be rumors."

But terrible rumors. Perhaps there is some terrible truth behind my father's warning. Perhaps we should refuse the case.

Pettigrew's father shook his head. "These may be figments of popular imagination, but they all point in the same direction: the Bulbul is a merciless and perverse killer. Perhaps he is even insane."

An insane killer. But it is too late to back out. It is now a matter of honor— we have accepted the task.

"Thank you, Father," Pettigrew said. "You have been most helpful."

Pettigrew Senior scratched his head and looked unhappily at Pettigrew and Flinders. "Are you really sure that you want to go on?"

Pettigrew nodded his head yes. Flinders nodded also.

"I do not know about the connection with the Hashshashin, but I would not be surprised. The Veiled One has many followers. He has turned all the ancient Islamic world to his will."

Pettigrew Senior pleaded once more, "My son, I do not want to lose you. And Flinders, you have so much to live for. Please abandon this madness." His fists curled tight, and the lines on his face were suddenly deeper.

"Father, I cannot."

"My son, you are a man. I bow to your will."

"You bow to my will? No, it is not about my will. Father, I do not want to go, but I must. I have made a promise—I have seen the hurt this killer has caused—and I am compelled to keep my word."

"You are decidedly a man, my son." Pettigrew Senior sighed and picked up his cigar. "You need to find Leonard Woolley. He can direct you further. I have known him for a long time and trust him entirely. He is excavating the site at Carchemish in Syria—Flinders, I am sure that you know all about it. It was a major city in antiquity going back to the Assyrians and Hittites. The British Museum has been excavating the palace complex for years."

Pettigrew Senior lit his cigar. Smoke curled around his head.

Flinders replied, "Yes, I spent almost a year studying Carchemish. Hogarth, who led the expedition before Woolley, lectured us on it. The finds there rival those at Ur of the Chaldees."

Pettigrew Senior smiled. "Woolley and I worked together for years. He helped me find burial sites in Egypt and Mesopotamia and put me onto some interesting Assyrian artifacts." He pointed to a small statue of a woman standing on a pedestal in the corner of the dining room. "That is Astarte. She is the Assyrian manifestation of the Sumerian Ishtar and the Egyptian Isis. Notice the serpent coiling around her."

An ancient myth.

"We have one like it."

The serpent image. This is where we began in Cairo.

Pettigrew Senior took a few puffs. "I will give you an introduction to Woolley. He is there now, along with Hogarth and one of Hogarth's students, a man named Lawrence. Lawrence is an expert on crusader castles. He has mapped them all, including the Krak des Chevaliers. He is a strange young man."

"Lawrence, you say," Flinders broke in. "I knew him at Oxford. He was studying to be an archaeologist. He was Hogarth's protégé. I think I was his only friend. He was very reclusive. We used to climb dormitory walls for sport. He ate nothing but bananas. I once saw him run a lighted candle along his arm. He said it was to build willpower. 'The trick, Flinders, is not minding when it hurts.'"

"Yes, I met him several times," Pettigrew said. "His father and mother were not married. Some said that the stigma distorted his personality. He was always riding around on a bicycle by himself. He never smiled."

Pettigrew Senior tapped his pipe on the table. "That is all I can tell you."

They left the dining room and walked back down the hall. The sphinxes watched them pass.

This may be the last time I walk down these halls.

"Don't forget your slickers," his father told them. He opened the front door, hugged Pettigrew farewell, and said again, "Please abandon this madness."

Then, in a soft voice, he added, "I lost your mother; I cannot bear to lose you."

As the cab pulled away, Pettigrew once again turned and looked through the small back window. Rain distorted his view; drops trickled down the window. He watched his father's figure become smaller in the distance and finally disappear in the mist, and he felt terribly lost.

Goodbye, Father. I may never see you again. You disappear, just like my childhood.

The cab stopped in front of the flat. The black door opened. Maggie beckoned them in and clucked when their shoes dripped water on her polished floor.

"I will purchase our steamer tickets," Flinders said. "We will go by packet to Latakia. It is an old Roman port on the Syrian coast—the Romans used to go there on holiday. Caesar and Cleopatra spent some time there. Then we will drive to Carchemish. Maggie will help us pack. Best that we arm ourselves."

"Caesar and Cleopatra?"

"Remember what my uncle told us on that warm morning." Flinders chuckled. "Caesar was the greatest womanizer of the Roman world. The Romans had a saying: 'Caesar is a husband to every woman, and a wife to every man.'" Flinders grinned. "But then he faced Cleopatra, and the game was over."

"Like Budge."

"Like Budge."

Flinders paused. "I think I should bring my old pistols."

The steamer trip was uneventful. The Mediterranean sparkled in greens and blues. Flinders strolled around the decks, smiled, and tipped his hat to the ladies in deck chairs. The ladies blushed and smiled back.

My friend, sometimes I envy you.

"I see that you haven't lost your touch," Pettigrew growled one afternoon while he watched Flinders smile and bow.

"You are a sour old fellow."

"Perhaps so. But aren't you a little old for this?"

Flinders smiled. "Like fine wine, some things improve with age," he responded.

Pettigrew rolled his eyes.

"You do remind me a little of a well-aged Bordeaux."

Flinders bowed to another young lady.

After what seemed to Pettigrew to be an eon, the steamer eased into port. Its horn honked proudly. The ladies cheered. Flinders smiled. Gangplanks lowered, and baggage handlers rushed up them. Heavy carts rattled back and forth. Waiting crowds shouted. Lines of cars appeared, and the greens and blues of the ocean turned into the duns and browns of the desert in front of them. The horizon was lost in a gray haze. A hawk circled black against the sun.

Pettigrew caught the sound of its shrill scream. *Looks unfriendly.*

FIVE

To Wake in the Desert

The gray car lurched across the uneven road along a line of low hills. Its yellow-spoked wheels spun in the dust. Its engine belched the smell of oil, and its wheels bumped and skittered as the car pitched and rolled. Its canvas top flapped and snapped in the wind. The road was no more than a rutted path—a path worn by successive caravans from time immemorial.

As the car descended into the plain, Pettigrew could see the desert below stretch out to infinity. "The sense of space here is different from that in England."

"In England, we are crowded together."

"Do you like being crowded together?"

"I'm used to it."

"Suppose you didn't have to be used to it?"

"I don't know." Flinders rubbed his nose. "Why are you suddenly philosophizing about crowds?" He turned up his collar. "It's hot, my nose is sunburned, the cart bounces like cricket ball, and you want to talk about crowds."

"What else is there to talk about?"

"Nothing—we are in the middle of emptiness."

As the car moved, the earth blended with the skyline. Squares of green foliage alternated with grayish-brown sand. A few dull brown buildings, tiny in the expanse, dotted the desert floor; their outlines quivered in the heat. Puffs of smoke, small whirlwinds, danced in the sunlight.

Pettigrew felt his shirt sticking to his back. His neck itched and burned. He pulled his wide-brimmed fedora lower over his forehead. He saw wavering white outlines of buildings on the bleak horizon. He heard the echo of people talking drift over the emptiness. His nose was dry from the dust. His lungs did not seem to work. Taking a deep, full breath was impossible.

"This part of Syria is really a steppe rather than a true desert," Flinders said, and he scratched his neck. "Before we left, I read Murray's *Handbook for Travelers in Syria and Palestine*. The little whirlwinds are called *giblis*. The large dust storms are known as *samuns*—poison winds. They are very dangerous." He sat up and pointed toward the cloudy distance. "Carchemish is over there. We will be there in about an hour."

As they drove, Pettigrew remembered his father's words: "Please abandon this madness."

Everything here looks dry and dead. Pettigrew saw nothing but emptiness in every direction. *Flinders is right; there is nothing here.*

The car descended into the plain. Pettigrew saw a line of ruins coming closer. Soon the ruins were on both sides of the car. They passed by half-buried buildings. Workers appeared, carrying shovels and pushing wheelbarrows. Men climbed in and out of pits. Other men wearing broad hats, stained shirts, and khaki shorts walked around piles of dirt and took notes on large clipboards. They talked with men in white turbans and gray robes. Horses dragged sledges alongside the car; their backs glistened with sweat. Drivers walked beside them and shouted. Dust covered everything and everyone. Dust dried Pettigrew's nose. He sneezed. Grit crawled on his skin. He rubbed his eyes.

The car stopped in front of a series of low, dirty-white tents, and a man in khakis and long brown socks stepped out from one of them. Pettigrew saw that he was thin, slightly round-shouldered, tanned to the point of leather, and had dark eyes and tight lips.

He is younger than I would expect for so famous a scholar.

"Good morning," the man said. He smiled, and the leather that was his face creased. He held out his hand. "I am Leonard Woolley. Thomas cabled me that you would be coming." He spoke with a London accent. "Do come in—it's hot outside." He led them into the tent. "I want you to meet two of my favorite people."

Dim light washed through the tent. When Pettigrew's eyes accustomed to the gloom, he saw a man and a woman smiling at him. The man was sitting on a leather ottoman and reading a book. The woman was standing over a small brazier. Woolley introduced the man. "This is T. E. Lawrence. He is here to help us and to complete his thesis on crusader castles."

Pettigrew shook the man's hand; it was covered with scars.

Curious. His hand is scarred, and his nails are bitten to the quick.

Pettigrew looked more closely. Lawrence was short, barely over five and a half feet tall, but heavyset like a wrestler. His eyes were piercing, and his nose was sunburned. His long face was set in a frown.

I wonder if he ever smiles, Pettigrew thought.

When he moved, blond hair fell down his forehead.

Curious. He is wearing an Oxford blazer as though he were still in college. Everyone else is in khakis. What kind of a man wears a blazer in the desert?

Lawrence put down his book. Pettigrew read the title: *Travels in Arabia Deserta.* Lawrence followed his eyes.

"Have you read this? It is by Doughty, a marvelous man much like myself—his origin is English, but his manners and dress are Arab. We both extol the Arab of the desert. You will also, in time."

So, this is the student who once went forty-five hours without food or sleep just to prove that he could do it.

Lawrence turned to Flinders. "Flinders, good to see you again. It has been a long time since Oxford. I have heard about your adventure with Cleopatra."

Flinders smiled, nodded, and shook Lawrence's hand.

"So you both have come to the desert. It will change you and strip away your London excesses." Lawrence abruptly sat down and returned to his reading.

His eyes, Pettigrew noted, were haunted.

There is something behind them, some terrible pain. They look at me, wide and blue and unreadable. Flinders knew him. Lawrence once told him that his mother beat him brutally, as if to break his spirit. What kind of a mother beats her son almost to death?

The woman stepped forward. "My name is Bell, Gertrude Bell." As she smiled and looked at Pettigrew, her eyes danced. She extended her hand.

She was tall for a woman, almost as tall as Pettigrew himself, but also very slim and fragile in appearance. Her hair was red and her eyes were green, and she was tanned from the sun. Her face was plain, and her nose was sunburned, but Pettigrew still thought her to be a handsome woman. Her lips were full, but pitted and dry, and Pettigrew thought that she must bite them. He could not read her eyes. Her handshake was strong, like a man's.

But she seems frail. I wonder . . .

Woolley smiled. "Miss Bell is here in her capacity as political officer. She is coordinating our efforts with the Ottoman governor. Every time we want to open up a new dig site, she gets permission from him."

"Do you speak Turkish?"

"Yes, Mr. Pettigrew, I speak it quite fluently."

Someone else once said that to me. I tried to make polite conversation. I said, "Your English is very good." She was offended. "Do not patronize me." I was crushed. A beautiful woman, possibly a daughter of Cleopatra, had spoken. I stared at the floor.

"And while we're on the subject, I speak Arabic and Farsi as well. And I read and write some German." She winked. "Do you have any questions?"

"I am impressed," he told her.

She smiled.

Woolley waved the detectives over to some ottomans. Their brown leather was worn. "You will have to excuse our accommodations. We are here temporarily until our house is ready." He laughed. "Mind you don't trip on the carpets—they're rumpled." He lit a cigar. "I have some brandy, if you would like. Do tell us why you're here. Thomas did not say much, just something about a jinn. And then we'll have dinner."

Everyone sat down. Woolley pulled at his cigar. Flinders explained the theft and the firman and the need to get to the Krak des Chevaliers to intercept the thief. He recounted what Pettigrew Senior had said about the Veiled One and the Bulbul Pasha. Lawrence listened attentively; a slight smile played on his face. Bell watched, her eyes expressionless. She lit a cigarette.

"Hashshashin, you say?" Lawrence's eyes twinkled. "Well, you certainly have got yourselves some formidable opponents." He closed the Doughty book and leaned forward. "There is a story, during the Crusades, that an assassin attempted to kill King Richard. The assassin slipped through a line of guards standing shoulder to shoulder and entered the king's tent. She stabbed Richard, but the dagger was turned by Richard's chain mail vest."

"She?"

"The assassin was said to be a woman."

Pettigrew smiled. "Do you recommend that we wear chain mail?"

Gertrude arched an eyebrow. "Perhaps you should be more careful around women, Mr. Pettigrew."

She has a tongue as sharp as a wasp's sting, thought Pettigrew.

"Just a thought, of course," she said. Her green eyes were roguish.

A large wasp.

Woolley examined his cigar. The tent was still. Flinders shuffled his feet. Then Lawrence spoke up.

"I also know something about your Aphrodite," Lawrence said. "I came across it in my research on crusader castles. The statue was known to the crusaders as the 'Serpent Woman.'" He stretched out his legs. "Baldwin found it in Constantinople during the First Crusade. He took it with him to Jerusalem when the crusaders conquered it. It remained there for a century." He leaned forward. "Baldwin III carried it with him when he marched with armor glittering and banners flying to meet Saladin at the Horns of Hattin. The crusader army was destroyed. Saracens searched the dead in the heat and the stench. They found the Serpent Woman and presented her to Saladin." He laughed. "There is a story that the knight who held the statue was feathered with arrows. His blood turned the pristine marble crimson. But when it was brought to Saladin, it was white again."

"Interesting," Gertrude said. She blew a smoke ring.

"As for your other villains, I do not know."

Woolley fiddled with his cigar case. Cigars spilled out onto the pock-marked brass tray that served as a table. "I have heard of them. They are like evil jinns, ancient creatures that feast on the lives of humans. It is said that the Veiled One drinks a cup of human blood every morning. And there are other stories too wild to be believed. Your search for Aphrodite may lead you to something more ancient, to more horror than you can imagine."

"Ghost stories." Lawrence snickered.

"Maybe so; maybe not," said Woolley. "These jinns may be all too real."

"I thought that jinns only popped out of bottles."

"Not these jinns."

Woolley leaned back and lit another cigar. Its smoke rose in the silence that followed. "Jinns are legendary creatures. They were made of smoke and fire. They shift shapes and appear at random." He blew a smoke ring. "They are ancient beyond belief. They are the essence of evil. And that may be what you will encounter here."

"Silly legends," Lawrence said with a laugh.

"Legends have a basis in truth."

Lawrence smiled. "Gertrude, what do you think?"

She snuffed out the cigarette. "Legends are legends." She sat back. "The jinns are an old South Arabian legend. I have seen photos of stellas depicting them. Horrible grinning figures with fangs and talons. The Koran says that Allah created them a thousand years before mankind."

"Were they a trial, then?" Flinders said. "Perhaps when Allah was modeling woman?"

Flinders, I admire your wit, but you're going to find your head in your hands. Remember what happened to John the Baptist when he made a joke about Salome.

She ignored him and lit another cigarette. "Are you so sure you want to take on these villains, Mr. Pettigrew?" She touched his arm.

Pettigrew nodded.

Her eyes twinkled. "Then you must be a mighty man indeed, Mr. Pettigrew." She laughed. "Are you such a mighty man, Mr. Pettigrew?"

He nodded. "I would like to think I am, in some ways."

She lowered her eyelids. "What woman could resist such a mighty man?"

Now what?

"Gertrude, those are old wives' tales," Lawrence broke in. "Tales mothers used to frighten their rebellious children."

Woolley chewed on his cigar. "Are you so sure?"

"Beings made of smoke and fire," Pettigrew murmured. "The Veiled One was made of smoke and fire."

"Even so," Flinders said. "We must go to meet them."

Lawrence put the book down. "So you want to go to the Krak des Chevaliers, do you? We are in the middle of Ramadan now. You haven't much time left. I will take you there. I am quite familiar with it. I mapped it for my study. It is two days' travel from here by car, longer if you go by horse or foot." He laughed. "I once walked across Mesopotamia, but we will go by car and then by horse. Can either of you ride?"

Mesopotamia, the land between the rivers—Lawrence says he had walked that land, but was it between the rivers or between fantasy and reality?

Pettigrew and Flinders nodded.

Lawrence leaned forward. "The Krak des Chevaliers is called a concentric castle because of its circles of round towers." Lawrence stretched. "I am an expert on crusader castles." He folded his arms. "The Krak was the headquarters of the Knights Hospitaller and the major Crusader fortification in Syria. It has enormous walls." He smiled. "They are said to be impenetrable." He laughed. "I climbed them once." He frowned and looked up. "I have climbed many walls. Yes, many walls, indeed." He rubbed his chin. "And I have many more to climb. The desert is my destiny."

A strange vision.

"Gertrude, please hand me one of your cigarettes." Lawrence grinned. "I don't usually smoke—I prefer chocolates—but under the circumstances . . ."

"You are becoming effete." She laughed and handed him the pack.

"I do not think so." He pulled out a cigarette and fumbled with it. "I am not used to the ways of men." He struggled with a match. "I do not like their crowded cities." He took a long pull at the cigarette. "I need space. The open road calls me. It must be long and straight, not crooked and hedged." He frowned. "I dislike curved roads. I think they will be the death of me."

"Is that why you are here?" Gertrude smiled. "We are kin, then."

"The desert is clean."

"Yes, the desert is clean." Gertrude nodded.

He laughed. "But enough of that. Your castle is now largely abandoned, but there are rumors that members of the Order of Assassins have been seen there." He smiled. "So you may be right." He pulled at his long gray socks. He wore red Persian shoes with curled up toes. "Yes, you may be right."

A strange costume. He affects Arab dress just like Lady Stanhope so many years ago.

The tent darkened as the sun went down. The noise of men and animals faded. "We must light the lanterns," Woolley said. "Lawrence, would you get out the lanterns?"

Their lights were spots of sudden brightness. Pettigrew looked away. Shadows danced on the canvas above him. Cigar smoke curled around him.

There is menace here; I can feel it in my bones. It is close by, but where?

Flinders asked, "How are we to get into it then?"

Lawrence sat back. "I know of an underground entrance. We can get in unobserved. There are only so many places where your exchange can take place. Most of the building is in ruins. We will start in the morning. It won't be easy."

He seems so sure.

Woolley broke in. "Dinner is ready. And then to bed. You have to get up early." He bent over the brazier and started filling plates. Everyone arranged themselves. Pettigrew sat on an ottoman. Gertrude sat cross-legged next to him. Her knee pressed against his. She leaned over the small fire and asked, "Would you like some of this lamb?" Her tousled hair brushed his face. He could smell her soft citrus scent. Her arm and breast touched him as she turned and handed him a plate. The low flames danced yellow and red in front of him. He saw Flinders out of the corner of his eye; Flinders nodded and grinned.

Flinders, you are a rogue.

After dinner, they talked. Gertrude told him how she had grown up in a wealthy family. How she had toured Persia as a young girl. "My uncle was ambassador to the Shah. I saw the wonders of the Middle East. I saw the glory of the desert." She laughed. "And now I am driven. I search for the horizon after the horizon."

"You sound like Flinders."

"Then your friend is a dreamer. He will soar like an eagle." She smiled and then frowned. "But I cannot soar. I am Icarus trapped in a woman's body. If I fly too close to the sun, I will burn and fall. I feel that I shall die, in despair, all alone in a dark room." She nodded to herself. "All alone, with only a bed and a table to comfort me."

"You will die all alone?"

"It is a dream that keeps recurring."

"There is no one?"

"There were many men, elegant, charming, and entitled. But they are only handsome feathers." She lit a match. "I could blow them over as easily as I blow out this match."

She blew out the match.

"You never married, then?"

"Mr. Pettigrew, you are impertinent." Her green eyes sparkled with amusement. "I need a man of granite, not a man of feathers." She leaned close, and the green eyes became mischievous. "Are you such a man?"

Am I such a man? Her eyes tease me.

"A man of granite?"

"Yes, a man that I could not blow over," she replied. The green eyes danced. "Let me show you something." She pulled a sheaf of photographs from a battered briefcase and spread them in her lap. She held one up. "My camera is my eye. My soul sees through its lens." She handed Pettigrew several photographs.

He examined them. "These are magnificent."

"I photograph everything that I see here."

"Is that you with a big hat on a horse?"

"Yes, someone else took that—it was in Iraq. I was in front of an ancient gate. Someday I will build a museum of antiquities."

She lit another cigarette. "I can blow smoke rings."

He smiled at her. "I thought only men could blow smoke rings."

"You are in error."

She smokes too much, he thought. *She has a nervous energy about her.*

"I see that you ride like a man."

"Of course." She grinned and fluffed her hair. "I can do anything a man can do." She laughed. "And quite often, much better."

He handed the photographs back.

The photographs were beautiful. But Pettigrew sensed there was some terrible secret behind the camera. Flinders had once said there were rumors about her father.

She took the photos and carefully put them in the briefcase. He saw a white scar that snaked down the brownness of her arm.

"How did you get that scar?"

"I was rock climbing, and I fell."

"Rock climbing? Rock climbing is dangerous. Women do not do rock climbing."

"I do."

"And you wander around in the desert, a woman alone. Even the great Lady Stanhope had forty bodyguards when she traveled."

She nodded. "But I am not Lady Stanhope."

"Are you not afraid?"

"No."

"Why not?"

She turned to him; her eyes were fierce. "The most degrading of human passions is the fear of death. I am not afraid of death."

Not afraid of death? Or wanting to die? Who is this woman?

Pettigrew looked into the dark eyes. *She sounds like Lawrence. There is something behind those eyes. Some terrible event that had warped her and driven her. Lawrence is clearly trying to prove his manliness because of his short stature. But Gertrude? I wonder what drives her. Did some man take advantage of her, and now she is forced to prove to the world that she is worthy? And worthy of what?*

They continued talking. An hour passed; then another. Their heads were close together.

She snuggled closer to him. "I feel your strength. Do you have someone?"

"There was someone once." He paused. "I miss her."

"I can sense that. You seem sad in a way." She brushed her hair back. "Everyone I might want to know better is always taken." She lit another cigarette, leaned back, and exhaled. "I do not know whether it is me or them." She stared into space for a moment and then laughed. "At heart, we are all lonely."

"Perhaps so."

She thought a moment. "Let me read you some Sufi poetry. Such poetry comforts me—I have translated many of Hafiz's poems." She pulled a small leather-bound book from her pocket. "Here is my favorite verse from Rumi." She read aloud in a soft voice:

> *There are many ways to the Divine.*
> *I have chosen the ways of Song, Dance,*
> *And Laughter.*

She closed the book, smiled, and looked at Pettigrew. Her eyes asked a question. His eyes answered.

"That is most beautiful. Is that how you feel about life?" Pettigrew took her hand.

"Yes."

But I do not believe her. There is a sadness beyond those green eyes. There is some terrible searching. Some void that no amount of song, dance, and laughter can fill.

For a long time, they sat in silence and watched the glowing coals. Then she stood up to leave. "Good night. I think you will find the desert exhilarating."

A short while later, Lawrence rose and said, "I must get ready for tomorrow." He turned as he left. "The desert cleanses us. You will see."

Woolley bid them good night.

Pettigrew watched the tent flap close. "They go to bed early," he said.

"Yes, very early."

"And they speak about the desert as if it were alive."

"It may be for them."

It seemed to Pettigrew that both of them were cleansing their souls in this desert, that they were using it as a flaming crucible, stripping away all vestiges of a past life and becoming austere and alone . . .

And clean. Forever clean. Curious. Most curious.

Woolley opened the tent flap. Pettigrew and Flinders stepped outside.

The sun had set; its white glare had faded to red and then disappeared. The wind had grown cool, and the air tanged of sage and other desert plants. Night birds began to chirp. The atmosphere softened to an orange dust before turning into the invisible clarity of night. The camp settled down; voices grew softer and movement slowed.

"Follow me," Woolley said. "I will show you to your tents."

Woolley walked slowly between the rows of tents. "Carchemish is the site of an ancient city. The Egyptians tried to conquer it; the Hittites defended it. The desert rumbled with the wheels of a thousand chariots. The earth ran red with blood."

He looked up at the stars that were creeping above them as the dust settled. "Sometimes at night, when the desert is still, I imagine I hear their war cries."

He puffed on his cigar. "And now we come like grave robbers to dig up their legacy." He threw down his cigar stub and rubbed it out. "The desert is an ancient place."

He scuffed the sand. "In the desert you hear things and see things that may have happened today or may have happened a thousand years ago." He smiled. "Reality is different here."

As they walked, Pettigrew felt the temperature change on the skin of his arms; the skin prickled with cold.

He was on the cricket field near his father's house. He could hear the tick of the bats and the calls of the players. He saw in his father's face, "You must come home."

A horse coughed, and the desert returned.

"Pettigrew, you take this one." Woolley opened a tent flap. "See that blanket? Use it. There is a mattress on the floor."

Pettigrew looked in. The tent was crowded with boxes; it looked uncomfortable, and it was still hot from the day's sun. "I think that I will sleep outside, if you don't mind."

Woolley nodded. "Flinders, you are over there."

"Good night."

Flinders was about to leave, but Pettigrew stopped him and pointed to the dark sky. Stars were beginning to appear, brighter and brighter until the whole sky became a blaze of cold light. "Flinders, do you remember when Holmes looked up at the starry sky?"

Flinders winced. "Surely you are not going to tell me that old joke again."

"Of course," Pettigrew continued in a hushed voice. "It is my solemn duty.

"Holmes looks up and says to Watson, 'Look up in the sky and tell me what you see.'

"'I see millions of stars.'

"'And what do you conclude from that, Watson?'

"'Well, it tells me that there are millions of galaxies and potentially billions of planets. It tells me that God is all powerful and that we are insignificant.'

"'Watson, you idiot, someone has stolen our tent!'"

A joke, but Watson may have been right. There is no comparison between the glory of the universe and the loss of a canvas tent.

"That was awful at Oxford," Flinders said, laughing, "and it has not improved at Carchemish. It brings back memories of insect specimens in bottles of cheap cognac and frog parts on chair seats."

"Not to mention moldy manuscripts and rotten mummy wrappings all over the floor." Pettigrew sighed. "It is a wonder that the dons didn't expel us."

A wonder indeed.

Flinders laughed and walked to his tent. Pettigrew stood in thought.

Such innocence, but we lost it long ago, and we can never recapture it, no matter how hard we try, or how much we joke and reminisce.

Pettigrew picked up the blanket Woolley had given him and walked around the outside of the tent. He found a spot that looked comfortable, spread the blanket, and gingerly lay down. The sand was soft. Slowly, he relaxed on the blanket. Its rough edges scratched his neck. Stars stretched above him, a glittering vault that he could reach out and touch. A vast emptiness. He felt the sense of unlimited expanse, as though his being was somehow alone in space. Sand moved and sung in his ears like the hum of a thousand bees.

A strange sound. Thousands of grains of sand in motion.

A chill wind blew fitfully across his face. He was in an endless world, a cypher in a vast shining universe—a universe that existed beyond his comprehension.

I feel as though I am alone in space. The stars beckon me. A cold wind from the stars blows in my face. I wonder how many have looked up at these stars before me and felt this unlimited expanse?

He shivered with the cold of the glitter above him, pulled the blanket close, and went to sleep. The camp became silent; somewhere a horse whinnied. Then all was still.

She came to him out of the darkness. She settled down beside him. He awoke. He felt her warmth in the cold as her body stretched along his. Her breath tickled his neck. His lips touched her cheek; his nose nuzzled her hair. Her touch excited him. He reached down and pulled at her belt and pants.

Strange, he thought, *how easily all these clothes come off. Clothes that look so fixed and important in the daylight.*

She lowered herself, carefully at first and then eagerly. He could see only a dark silhouette moving against the shining stars.

In his mind, a voice—her voice—asked, "Is it her or me?"

Another voice answered—his voice. "Why do you ask? You know the answer."

"It has been a long time."

"Time means nothing."

"I want to know."

The second voice answered, "It is you."

The first voice continued, "Are you sure?"

"Yes, it will always be you. You are the only woman that I have loved. There will be no others."

"I will wait for you, my love."

"I will come to you."

The voices stopped.

An old memory came back. *Cairo was dark. The cobbled street was rough under his boots. "This is an ancient street, one that was built by the Fatimids." She danced before him. His eyes never left her. A door opened, and light spilled onto the cobbles. Music blared and people laughed. She spoke. "I dance very well. I will dance with you if you like." Their eyes met. And then she died. But that was so long ago.*

The vault that was the sky above him shone with a terrible and vast emptiness.

It feels so lonely. I am so lonely.

Pettigrew remembered snatches of a poem; the verses marched in his mind. *How did they go?*

> *A book of verses.*
> *A jug of wine.*
> *A loaf of bread.*
> *And thou beside me,*
> *Singing in the wilderness.*
> *I am in the wilderness now, but where are you?*

The question remained unanswered.

The desert wind hummed in his ears. The vault shone. He dozed off. She was in his arms; he could feel her breathing as he slipped into sleep. In the morning, she was gone. He woke up alone in the desert. The vault was still above him but fading in the swelling sunlight; the smell of rock and sage was all around him. A green lizard poked its head out from under a dried bush, fixed him with its obsidian eyes, and then darted out of sight. As the sun rose, the sky turned to a pale buttermilk lined by pink clouds.

He watched as the night shadows turn into ochre and gold.

What was it that Gertrude had said? "To wake in the desert dawn was like waking in the heart of an opal."

She was right, but his back was stiff and bruised by the desert pebbles. He picked up the blanket, rolled it up, and went back to his tent. He curled up on the mattress and slid off to sleep.

An hour or so later, Flinders lifted the tent flap, and the sound woke him. Flinders looked in and grinned at him. "I see that you have had an interesting night. And so soon. Miss Bell is all smiles this morning."

Pettigrew got up slowly, feeling the bruises and remembering the woman. He could still taste her lip rouge.

The tent was dark and drab after the starry night. Flinders stepped through the tent flap and smoothed his hair. "Thomas, these people are not what they seem. I had a long talk with Lawrence last night"—Flinders laughed—"while you were busy with Miss Bell."

He turned serious and went on. "Bell and Lawrence are using Woolley as cover while they map out Ottoman fortifications. They all work for British Intelligence. Lawrence's thesis research on crusader castles is really an excuse to travel around Syria and get access to military installations." Flinders paused. "Thomas, we have gotten ourselves into the middle of a clandestine enterprise."

"So Gertrude is really a spy?"

"Yes, they all are."

She seems so alive, yet so fragile. No, not fragile, but supple, like a Damascus blade that flexes before it strikes. The imagery of the blade suits her. The green eyes haunt me.

"That is not our business," Pettigrew said. "We are here to recover Budge's statue."

"They are planning for a war."

"Then we must hurry, before it starts."

Will the desert sear us also in the days to come? Pettigrew rubbed his eyes. *I wonder.* Then he rummaged around and packed his belongings. He lifted the tent flap and walked into the bright sun. The car with its bright yellow spokes was pulled around, the driver was instructed, and their luggage was loaded. Lawrence added a few bags and then closed the trunk. He had changed into khakis.

"A picture before you go," Woolley said. He held up a large camera. "Come on, give me some big smiles."

Flinders, Pettigrew, Lawrence, and Bell hugged each other and mugged for the camera. Gertrude stood next to Pettigrew. Her arm was tight around his waist. He could feel her shiver.

"I will be all right," he whispered. "We will meet again."

The photograph over, they broke apart.

Lawrence smiled and said, "As I said, the desert is clean. Now we shall experience its cleanliness."

They climbed into the car—Lawrence in front, Flinders and Pettigrew in the rear. The driver started his engine.

"Wait." Woolley went over to a wooden carton stacked on the side of a tent. He opened its hatched lid and pulled out three dun-gray machine pistols and several boxes of cartridges.

"You might need these."

SIX

A Desert Has No Footpaths

The gray car slipped in sand and bounced off rocks. A snake's tail of dust and dirt billowed behind it. A canvas water bag hung from the hood and banged fitfully against its radiator. The car's canvas top rattled; dust flew off it and circled the car. Pettigrew pulled the scarf tighter around his nose, but the dust got through it anyway. Dry paper filled his mouth. His neck burned and he pulled the fedora's wide brim lower. He looked out—fitful columns of dust danced in lines on the desert floor.

A ballet of dust in the dryness. What was it Gertrude said? He remembered her words: "There is a certain fine simplicity in a landscape from which all water is missing." *The clarity of vision here is truly stark, but I miss the softness and fog of England.*

"Damn, I think I have been bitten by a flea." Pettigrew scratched a bite.

Lawrence laughed. "There are fleas everywhere, even in the desert."

So much for philosophy.

The car bounced along. The desert became a scorching furnace. Pettigrew opened his collar. His hair was limp. His skin felt on fire.

This is a furnace. A furnace to burn away all civilized adornments. We now come to the brutal and simple meaning of life.

Lawrence turned in his seat and followed Pettigrew's eyes. "You look out at the desert, and you wonder." He pointed into the expanse. "The desert is

like an ocean in which no oar had been dipped. It exists there, all unknow-
ing and unknowable."

He added, "It could become a terrifying weapon." His eyes widened.
"Just think. A Western army needs roads and garrisons. The bedouin need
nothing."

"You have become a military strategist?" Flinders laughed. "A desert
Von Clausewitz, perhaps?"

"You do not see." Lawrence frowned. "A Western army is like a flower;
its head has teeth, but its stem is weak." Lawrence stared into the horizon. "The bedouin would attack the stem. The Western soldiers would sit
on their posts, squinting into the emptiness. And then, the attack out of
nowhere." He laughed, embarrassed by his eloquence.

"Ah, such grand thoughts," Flinders said, winking at Pettigrew, "from
one so young."

Lawrence scowled. "War is a serious business."

So you would turn this expanse into a war zone.

"That may be true," Pettigrew said. "But fortunately we are not here to
engage in war—we are here merely to recover a statue."

"I may write a book about military strategy in the desert." Lawrence
looked thoughtful for a moment. "Yes. The desert is a sea, and camels are
its warships."

"So it is." Flinders smiled and pulled his hat over his nose.

They drove all day through the heat. The desert shimmered; the giblis
twirled. Pettigrew was wet with sweat. Flinders curled into a damp lump
beside him. Lawrence twisted in his seat; his blue eyes twinkled. "We travel
in the heat of day. The bedouin are much more sophisticated. They travel at
dawn and evening and rest during midday."

"Indeed." Flinders sat up. "I'm told they use the stars as guides."

"Yes, they write their wills across the stars and the sand."

Flinders said something like that once.

"Let us stop and have some water. Water is precious here; you will soon
learn to appreciate its worth."

Lawrence told the driver to stop. The car stopped, and they drank from
the bag. The water was cool.

"The bedouin are always thirsty. They use water only for cooking and to cleanse themselves for prayer." Lawrence tilted the bag.

When the car started again, Lawrence leaned back and spoke to them. "The bedouin blend into the desert; they become one with it. But we arrogant Englishmen attempt to overpower it." He turned back to the front and peered through the grimy windshield. "Only an hour or so before we can rest for the night."

The sun set, and the world descended into darkness. The car drove through several villages, its headlights winding around crooked corridors as they passed through the tiny clusters of civilization. Pettigrew's eyes searched for life. Nothing human moved; the stillness was complete. Walls appeared out of nowhere and then flashed by into the dark. Overhead, Ottoman porches rippled past; their latticework screens were dark. Their cupolas were barely visible as the car slid by.

Not a light anywhere. These porches overhang the street like the curled arches in a Gothic cathedral.

A white bird flew over the car's hood and hovered motionless in front of the windscreen. Its yellow eyes, two blank circles, were magnified by the glass. Its open beak was a black void. The bird stared at them and then flew over the car. Pettigrew threw his arms up to protect his face. *A bird or an omen?* He heard a dog bark. The bark reverberated from the shifting walls and lost itself in the distance.

The loneliness is oppressive, thought Pettigrew. *The streets are empty. There is a sense of menace. Does anyone live here?*

They stopped outside a village, ate a small dinner, and unrolled their sleeping bags. Pettigrew propped his head against a tire. Some of its dust fell on his face. He brushed it off. His neck hurt; the tire was hard and unforgiving. The heat turned cold, and Pettigrew's wet clothes felt like ice, even inside the blanket. The sand buzzed. He heard voices echoing from nowhere. The vault turned above him—thousands of stars marching against the dim line of the horizon.

I feel dizzy when I look up. If I move, I may fall off the end of the earth.

He slid into sleep.

The sun rose, and the car started with a blast of sound and fury. Its wheels spun in the sand as it rumbled forward. It became a crawling black insect outlined by a blaze of pink and orange light on a barren plain.

An opal indeed.

Many searing hours later, they encountered sheep, goats, and camels in front of them; their shapes were black outlines against the red of the setting sun. As the car drew abreast, Pettigrew watched lines of horses and camels packed with baggage plodding forward.

They move endlessly.

Men in gray and women in black walked between the animals. The men carried bags and guns. Many of the women had babies strapped to their backs and held small children by the hands. Their shadows trailed behind and shimmered in the ruts of the road. Cries of camel drivers punctuated the sound of moving flocks. Clouds of dust puffed over men, women, and animals—phantoms moving in the haze.

The desert was alive with their movement.

Lawrence studied the caravan. "They are Ruwallah. They are migrating in search of water; they are much farther north than usual. They follow the sun."

He looked thoughtful for a moment and then said, "I have an idea. Let me speak to their shaykh and find out where they are going. They may provide us with cover to approach the castle." He gestured. "Driver, stop the car." He got out and disappeared into the dust.

The car stopped, and the caravan receded. Flinders and Pettigrew exchanged looks. Then, out of the dust, a figure appeared. The car growled to a start, lurched forward, and stopped. Lawrence got in.

"They will make camp on the plain below the Krak," he said. "When they set up camp, we will go to the castle. The shaykh will lend us horses. In the meantime, we must become part of the migration. It is another two days' march." He opened the car door. "Let us join them. They have welcomed us. We will walk with them."

The three got out and walked with the bedouin. Pettigrew could sense, rather than see, the men and women around him, spectral figures outlined in brown, all moving in unison. Shouts echoed in his ears; chatter flowed around him. Camels burped over his head.

We move as one. We have become one with them—walking, walking, end-less walking in the dust.

The gray car slowly followed; its exhaust sputtered in the dust. The yellow spokes were black with grime.

A shout signaled the end of the march; the walkers and riders spread out. The camp was swiftly set up; black tents grew out of the desert floor. Animals were herded into compact clusters. Cooking fires dotted the fading light. The smell of meat and spices filled the night air. Time passed slowly as the sun became a sullen red disk and sank out of sight. The horizon streamed with pinks and oranges. The noise of men and animals subsided. The camp became silent in the night. Tiredness overwhelmed Pettigrew, and his eyes closed; the vault shone through his lids. The tire was hard, and the sand was scratchy.

Then came the blackness of sleep.

Pettigrew woke up in the morning light. A small woman in black with long braids and kohl-darkened eyes was standing over him. She smiled and held out a cup. She poured steaming coffee from an hourglass-shaped pot with a parrot's beak and offered it to him.

"You are honored," Lawrence said, grinning. "She offers you coffee. Because you are not a believer, you are not required to fast. She is the shaykh's daughter. She says that she watched you walk. She has never seen such a man as you. You are a giant with hair the color of lemons in the sun. She wants to know if you are taken."

"Are you taken?" a voice spoke in his head.

"I don't know."

"Are you so sure that you don't know?"

"I am not sure."

"You are sure. Tell her the truth."

Pettigrew rubbed his forehead.

"So"—Flinders appeared out of nowhere—"the sleeping prince is awakened by the beautiful maid. Maybe we should have music and dance."

Lawrence grinned. "But here they do debka."

Pettigrew sat up, smiled, and took the cup from the woman. Their hands touched under it. The coffee was dark and hot. He smiled at her and then turned to Lawrence.

"Tell her that she is a princess among women, more beautiful than the morning sunrise, more perfect than the moon against the stars. Tell her that my heart would go out to her, but alas, I am betrothed to another."

"You learn swiftly, my friend. You could be a bedawi after all." Lawrence laughed. "There is a proverb: 'Even a one-eyed man winks at a woman.'"

Flinders laughed too. "Astonishing. Thomas, I had no idea you were so eloquent." He struck a pose. "Maybe those acting lessons would have been a good idea."

Lawrence spoke to the woman in Arabic. She smiled and set the coffee-pot down. Her perfume was a faint scent of flowers in the desert air. As she straightened, she gave Pettigrew a long look and then turned and left. Her long braids swung, and her bracelets jingled as she walked away. Pettigrew watched the swing of her braids and the sway of her hips.

What kind of woman is that who demands to know whether I am taken?

Pettigrew sat up and drank the coffee. It was bitter and strong.

"There is another matter," Lawrence said. He looked serious. "The shaykh asks your help. I told him that you are a doctor. He said that several of his people are sick, and a number of women are in childbirth."

The shaykh asks my help—now, that is something.

"I did not bring my bag. There is not much that I can do, but lead the way." He rolled up the sleeping bag and followed Lawrence. "Flinders, come along—I may need your assistance."

They walked among the tents. Women in black and men in gray stared at them.

They see us as curiosities, beings from another world who have suddenly appeared.

Pettigrew nodded and smiled. The Ruwallah did not smile back.

To them we are Sanger's freaks, and our dress is an affront to their eyes.

He saw the woman with the braids. She stood apart. Her arms were folded; she did not smile, but her eyes glowed.

Flinders muttered, "I feel that I am marching down the street at Tombstone."

"To the paddock?"

"Corral."

The shaykh met them outside a large tent. He spoke softly and with a London accent. "Please help my people."

"Of course, but I have no medicine."

"I understand. God will guide your hand."

I wonder.

"He speaks perfect English," Pettigrew whispered to Lawrence as they went into the tent.

"His father had him educated in England," Lawrence replied. "He could have stayed in England and lived the life of a fine gentleman, but he returned to his tribe."

Several women sat on a carpet. One woman was crying. A small boy lay under a blanket; he was very pale.

Pettigrew examined him. "His arm is infected. It needs cleaning. There is no medicine." He turned to Lawrence. "Is there any soap and water here?"

"No, they clean themselves with sand."

"With sand?"

"They use water only to drink and to wash before prayers."

A waterless world. No rain, no fog, no mist. A world that would be incomprehensible from my sitting room in London.

Pettigrew shook his head. "Let them try one of their poultices. It may work. He is young and strong."

He left the tent, and immediately a crowd of women and children surrounded him.

"Word of your presence has spread," Lawrence said.

They follow me. Their eyes search my soul. I am only a man.

Pettigrew spent the day soothing sick children and delivering babies. "They use traditional herbs," he told Flinders when he stepped out of one of the tents. "They close wounds by filling them with fire ants. Fire ants, Flinders! They treat people with heart conditions by burning their chests with cigarettes. There is no hygiene. Florence Nightingale would be horrified."

Women and children followed him as he walked from tent to tent. They called out to him, pleading.

"What can I do?" he said wearily to Flinders. "I am only a physician, not a magician."

"To them, you are both, and perhaps more than that."

"Perhaps I don't want to be a magician."

Pettigrew walked and examined and prescribed. In some tents, he shook his head hopelessly; in others, he smiled. He thought he saw the woman with the braids watching him. The women followed him; they pushed their children at him.

"Now for the babies. The mothers will remain fully dressed," Lawrence said. "Bedouin modesty prevents them from undressing in front of strangers. A female relative will be present. Pettigrew, you can go in alone. The shaykh has decreed that because you are a doctor."

"What do you want me to do?" Flinders asked as he patted a small boy on the head.

"I will deliver the babies," Pettigrew replied, "and you will hand them to the midwives outside the tent. And mind you don't drop one."

"I'm not sure I can do that."

"Nonsense."

The babies cried. Flinders sweated. The midwives laughed.

"Flinders, you have the instincts of a physician."

"No, I have the instincts of a father."

The day was long with hope and despair.

In one of the tents, Pettigrew frowned and picked up a baby.

"See this?"

The baby's lips were not joined; he was deformed. He held it out to Flinders. "He has a harelip, and his palate is cleft. In London, this harelip would be sutured before the mother even saw it. But here, there is no hope. He will be terribly disfigured."

Flinders took the baby and cradled the infant in his arms. His eyes teared.

Lawrence spoke. "Children will laugh at him and call him 'the hideous one.' They will laugh and taunt him."

"His life will be misery."

Like Sanger's freaks.

Lawrence frowned. "That cannot be helped—we have no say here."

Flinders rocked the baby and whispered, "You do not deserve this. No one asks to be deformed."

"Give him to them." Lawrence was insistent.

Flinders handed the baby to the midwives. They peered at it and clucked to themselves.

"The shaykh may decide not to let it live," Lawrence said. "There is no place here for him."

"No place?" Flinders's face crumpled in shock.

"This is a hard world, a world without mercy. Survival is the basic rule. Everyone must contribute or go." Lawrence frowned. "One way or another."

"Then I will adopt him and take him home." Flinders started toward the midwives.

Lawrence put a hand on his shoulder. "You cannot."

"Flinders, you cannot save the world." Pettigrew put a hand on his shoulder and they began walking to another tent.

Flinders lagged behind. Pettigrew saw him turn and watch the midwives as they carried the baby into a tent. The baby was crying. The tent flap closed.

And maybe you cannot save yourself.

Outside of the last tent, a young mother pushed her son at him. Lawrence translated her words. "His name is Adl—it means justice. His mother says that he is sick and cannot water the camels."

Pettigrew saw a tall boy of about fifteen in front of him. The boy looked unhappy. His mother twisted her thawb; the long gown fluttered. The boy stood in front of Pettigrew. He did not smile.

"Come here," Pettigrew said. He listened to the boy's chest. He felt under the boy's jaw. "Tell him to stick out his tongue." Pettigrew looked. "This boy is fine." He ruffled the boy's hair. "Send him back to the camels."

The mother smiled. The woman with the braids laughed.

Lawrence applauded. "You have given him justice. You could become a qadi, a judge to decide the truth."

A qadi? A judge to decide the truth? How am I to know the truth about anything?

Lawrence led them to a tent. "The shaykh has given us this for the night."

Pettigrew entered and collapsed on a rug. Flinders sat on a cushion beside him.

"There are pillows and beds," Lawrence said in surprise. "The shaykh is lavish in his hospitality."

"How so?"

"The bedouin sleep on the bare ground with only blankets," Lawrence said. "They do not use such luxuries."

"A hard people."

"The desert is hard." Lawrence looked at Flinders. "You cannot make life soft for them." He paused. "And even if you could, they would not accept it."

"Not to accept modern civilization?"

"You do not understand the bedouin. They are a people bound together by family, honor, and blood vengeance."

"Blood vengeance?"

"I will tell you a story." Lawrence closed his eyes. "Once there was a murder. The offended tribe sought vengeance. They rode out and found a small boy. The boy saw them and was afraid. He put his thumbs in his mouth as a sign of surrender. He cried. The men looked at each other. 'He is a boy—why should we kill him?' the leader said. 'Honor requires a life,' and he plunged his dagger into the boy's heart."

For a moment there was silence.

"I need a drink."

Flinders reached into a worn valise and pulled out a flask.

"Where did you get that?"

Flinders grinned. "Remember when we went to Edinburgh to attend Bell's lectures? Bell taught us in his criminology class, 'Preparation, preparation, and preparation.'"

They raised their glasses. "To a hard people."

"No," Flinders said. He held his glass high. "To a small baby."

The glasses clinked.

The next morning, Lawrence said, "And now we must dress for the part." He handed Flinders and Pettigrew gallabiyahs. "The shaykh has provided us with bedouin garb. Take these."

Pettigrew put on the gallabiyah over his khakis and the kufiyah, the headdress, over his bare head. Lawrence handed him a leather belt with a curved dagger and stood back.

Pettigrew fingered the cords on the kufiyah. "Curious."

"They are a symbol of manhood. Today, you are a man."

"Am I truly? Because I don these articles of clothing?"

"Let me look at you. Ah, yes, you are indeed formidable. We shall call you 'Abul hol.'"

"Abul hol?"

"'Father of Fear.' It is the name of the Great Sphinx. What do you think, Flinders?"

Flinders laughed and turned his head from side to side. "I agree. He is Thutmose incarnate."

Pettigrew flexed his arms in the gown. "These clothes speak of a different reality," he said.

"Indeed, they do," Flinders answered.

Flinders and Lawrence put on their robes. Lawrence strode back and forth and admired himself. "Today I wear gray, the color of a badu; tomorrow I will wear white, the color of a prince. I will be a prince of disorder. I will write my will across the sky and stars."

Curious, very curious. He struts and frets. I wonder if the desert will prove a good stage for him. He is lost between two worlds. For him, the times are out of joint.

Another thought came. *Perhaps the time is out of joint for us as well.*

Flinders watched, noncommittal. Then he grinned. His eyes twinkled. "These garments feel heavy to me. Perhaps they need some tailoring."

Lawrence turned and frowned.

"Do not be deceived. Their weight absorbs the heat; their looseness allows the air to circulate."

The morning shadows shortened as the sun rose. The sky flowed from pink to pale blue. The camp came to life around the three of them. Men, women, and children came out of the black tents, laughing and talking.

They all know one another; they have a bond that is lost to us "civilized" Englishmen.

"They have a bond," Pettigrew commented.

"Of course. They are all related," Lawrence said. "They marry their brothers and sisters and other relatives."

They are all related; they are one family.

"How do you like your dagger?"

Pettigrew pulled the dagger from its sheath. Its blade blinded him as he twisted it.

It is blinding; it is the desert sun itself. An ancient weapon for an ancient people. Its blade is sharp like that of a razor, just as the people are like razors in this harsh landscape. I wonder if I could survive here.

"There is an inscription on its blade. Lawrence, what does it say?"

"Let the Sword Decide."

"Let the sword decide"—a fitting motto for a hard people.

Pettigrew carefully put the knife in its sheath. Its handle fit his hand as though it were made for him. His fingers caressed its knurls.

Curious, most curious. This blade becomes one with me; it is a living thing. But I wonder if I could use it on another.

"And now for transportation. We will send the car back to Carchemish and use camels. We will become Ruwallah. No one will notice us. We have one more day's march." Lawrence straightened and placed his hands on his hips. "Come, let us find our steeds."

"Camels, you mean." Pettigrew frowned. "I don't like camels."

Lawrence led them to a makeshift pen where a line of camels was tethered on a long rope. Men and boys were saddling the camels. Dust flew about amidst the shouts. Camels trotted back and forth. Pettigrew strode into the enclosure.

Might as well make the best of this.

He saw a row of kneeling camels. "They don't look very friendly," he said to Flinders.

"Would you?" Flinders replied.

Lawrence pushed Pettigrew toward a dun-colored camel with a red saddle. "She is a female and easy to ride." The camel burped.

"She smells bad, and I don't like the look in her eye," Pettigrew said. "But I'll give it a try."

Lawrence propelled him into the saddle. "Sit tall. Good. Now you look like a shaykh." The camel lurched up.

Whoa, I'm getting dizzy from all this swaying. This damn thing is going to tip over, and I'm going to break something when I fall off.

The camel began an unsteady walk. Pettigrew clung to the saddle.

When I was a boy, my father put me on a horse. I held on tight.

"Lawrence, are you sure this beast won't trip?"

The sky swirled overhead.

I think I am going to be sick.

The ground heaved; the faces at the fence blurred. The camel burped again.

"Wonderful!" Lawrence shouted. "You could be Caliph Omar himself, charging the unbelievers."

That's easy for you to say.

The camel swayed and Pettigrew swung from side to side in the saddle.

I think I'm getting a nosebleed from the height; the ground looks a long way down. Will this awful feeling never stop?

But it did stop.

Slowly the camel's gait smoothed out. Pettigrew sat up in the saddle. He tapped the camel with his stick. The pace quickened; the strides became longer. Dust flew in all directions. Rope fences flashed by. Moments passed.

Let me rethink this. This camel is magnificent; we could ride for eternity.

Pettigrew reined the camel to a halt and looked around. The rope fence was crowded with women and children. They laughed and yelled, "Ya, ya, Abul hol."

He looked closer. The woman who had offered him coffee was in the middle of the children. She watched him, her eyes serious. She smiled, but she did not laugh. Pettigrew turned the camel and rode along the fence to where she stood. He looked down. Their eyes met.

The march began. A line of camels plodded out of the enclosure. Pettigrew could feel them on both sides. Sometimes his knees rubbed against those of other riders. Camels loaded with baggage followed. Women and children walked next to him. Horses, sheep, and goats strung out behind him. He turned to look. Walkers, camels, horses, and sheep stretched as far as his eyes could see.

I can feel the energy and the excitement. We are hundreds, but we move as one.

They walked the whole morning. They rested during the heat of the day. Then they marched some more. Pettigrew slumped over in his saddle, lulled by the camel's rhythmic movement. They set up camp late in the evening.

"Normally, they would travel longer into the night," Lawrence said, pulling his camel alongside Pettigrew's. "But the shaykh says that his people are tired; they have come a long way and must rest." He grinned. "And besides, we are invited to dinner. The shaykh is keen to meet you. He thinks that he may have been at Oxford when you were a student there. You have cut quite a figure, 'Abul hol.'"

The camel knelt. Pettigrew got off and gave her a kiss on the nose. The camel burped.

Lawrence looked puzzled. "I thought that you hated camels."

"I do. But Nellie is different."

"Nellie, is it? I thought her name was Ayisha."

"She is Nellie to me."

"You have the heart of a bedawi, my friend."

Flinders rode up and dismounted. "I see you and the camel have become friends. Perhaps we should reconsider the circus." He laughed. "Possibly you could find an elephant that you fancy. Perhaps even Jumbo himself."

That evening, they went to the shaykh's tent. The tent was crowded with men in dark robes. The shaykh sat at the head of a long mat. His sons sat on both sides. Women placed large trays on small stands; the tent smelled of meat and spices. The woman with the braids served coffee. Pettigrew could not take his eyes off her. Her hair was down, and she wore a glimmering white abayah. As she leaned close to pour the coffee, he saw the dark eyes accentuated by kohl and smelled the heavy perfume. Again, their eyes met.

She is beautiful. Who is this woman who serves me coffee?

"What is her name?"

The shaykh, a small man with a graying beard, laughed. "Her name is Unayza. She is my oldest daughter, and she insisted on serving you. What am I to do? I am only a man. My sons would obey me; my daughters will not."

He looked fondly at his daughter. "Unayza is a famous name from an ancient qasidah about the desert. When I was young, I would recite these poems to my wife. Listen: this one is by Imrul Qays; it is most famous:

> *Stop, oh my friends, let us pause to weep over the remembrance*
> *of my beloved.*
> *Here was her abode on the edge of the sandy desert between*
> *Dakhul and Huwmal.*
> *The traces of her encampment are not obliterated even now.*
> *For when the South wind blows the sand over them, the North*
> *wind sweeps it away.*

"It is a beautiful poem," Flinders said.

"Yes, it is haunting. When my daughter was born, we named her Unayza after the poet's love. Unayza was a woman whom the great poet worshipped and lost. Pray that my daughter will not become someone's lost love." His eyes followed his daughter as she served coffee to Pettigrew.

Pettigrew looked up at Unayza. She bent down to fill his cup. Her hair trickled down the side of his face. Her presence intoxicated him. "Yes, pray."

Lawrence watched and murmured to himself, "Be careful what you do, my friend."

A tray of lamb and vegetables was set before Pettigrew. "Use only your right hand and do not reach across the serving in front of you." Lawrence's words echoed in his ear. "You must be polite. Just follow what I do."

After dinner, the conversation turned to the Veiled One. Flinders again explained what had happened in the museum.

"I have been there and seen the exhibits," the shaykh said simply, when Flinders had finished.

"We saw with our own eyes what he did there—what he is capable of," Pettigrew replied. "But we need to know more. What manner of man do we face?"

The shaykh fingered his prayer beads and muttered a prayer under his breath. "I have heard of him whom you seek. He rampages in the land and turns the sown into desert. They say he changes shape and becomes an animal."

The beads clicked.

Pettigrew put his cup down and looked at Unayza. Her eyes were wide with worry.

"They say he attacks and kills whole villages and destroys their herds." The shaykh murmured a prayer. "My people once came upon such a village. Bodies of men, women, and animals were everywhere. There was no sound except the wind. There was only dirty smoke, pale death, and blackbirds feeding. The smell of decay was in our noses for days." The shaykh put his beads down. "I personally do not believe in jinn. But if there was ever someone who could be called a jinn, it would be the Veiled One. All the tribes live in fear of him."

Flinders said, "We must go to meet him anyway."

"You should be very careful then."

"We are determined."

"I will give you two men. They will think you are looking for wells."

"We are honored." Pettigrew spoke to the shaykh, but out of the corner of his eye, he saw Unayza. Her eyes were dark.

"Shukran, thank you."

The shaykh smiled.

"Your men can stay with the camels; we will go alone to the castle."

"Hamdullah, praise God." The shaykh fingered his beads. "I will pray for you." He touched his heart.

The dinner ended, and they went back to their tents. Pettigrew tossed and turned. The image of Unayza hung in this mind. He remembered the shaykh's words. "Pray that she does not become someone's lost love."

They left the camp the next day in the late afternoon.

The camels plodded silently. Pettigrew saw the sharp outline of the castle—an enormous blackness against the flash of the sun. Its crenelated walls were jagged teeth against the brightness. Pettigrew stared in awe.

Who were these men that created such an edifice? What sweat and toil did they endure?

They picked their way up the rocky hillside and reined their camels in under the ruined ramparts. Pettigrew sensed the immense weight of the castle—the weight of centuries past.

How many battles were fought here? he wondered. *Did this hill run with blood and cries? Was the air dark with arrows?*

"We will stop here and go on foot," Lawrence said, dismounting from his kneeling camel. "There is a tunnel entrance not far from here. I mapped it a year ago." He led them to a massive tower. "We must hurry—the sun is beginning to set. Stay close to the wall; you will be more difficult to see."

The stone wall was warm in the heat. It shimmered before Pettigrew's eyes. The sun's rays bounced off the crumbling limestone, patches of green gave off a dusty smell, and twigs crunched under Pettigrew's feet.

"This is the outer ring—the entrance is over there." Lawrence's eyes searched the wall. "Ah, there it is. Well hidden. It was a sally port to allow defending knights to catch attackers by surprise." He pointed. Pettigrew saw a low opening covered by an iron grate.

Defending knights? Did they emerge, banners waving, shields clashing, and charge the enemy? Did the Cross of Jerusalem float red and white over their heads? Did they shout and slash? What is this place?

The grate was covered with rust. Lawrence and Flinders pulled it open. The hinge squealed; rust stained their hands. One by one, they crawled through. Light became dark.

Pettigrew's eyes were slow to adjust. A narrow tunnel opened before him. Fading sunlight streamed from behind him and rippled over uneven flagstone slabs. Vacant doorways opened on either side. Puffs of chill air and a sour smell hit him as he passed. Pettigrew imagined that he heard cries and screams from the openings. Despair reached out to him.

It is dark and cold here. The coldness hurts my bones.

Lawrence pushed ahead, leading them down the tunnel. "This is the dungeon level. We must ascend to the great hall. It is one of the few rooms left intact after an earthquake centuries ago. The exchange will probably take place there."

Pettigrew stumbled on. He could barely see in the dim light.

The tunnel ended in a round tower. A narrow flight of broken steps led up one wall. Pettigrew could not see the upper end of the steps; they disappeared in the gloom.

These go up to nowhere.

"Stay close to the wall, and don't look down," Lawrence warned them and started climbing. Flinders followed.

Pettigrew hesitated. "First camels, now rock climbing."

This feels like a scene from The Master of Ballantrae. *I hope we don't just step into empty space.*

Flinders looked back. "Nonsense. Consider this a physical fitness exercise."

After what Pettigrew thought was an eon, they reached the top and climbed onto a level floor. Darkness became a cloudy gloom.

"This part is better preserved," Lawrence told them. "The great hall is this way." They hurried down a mullioned corridor.

Pettigrew imagined he could see shadowy figures in chain mail standing along the walls. They held spears and shields; their eyes were sightless. They stretched in front of him in a ghostly line. The dim light filtered through their bodies. *My mind can hear the clink of armor and see white vestments emblazed with red crosses.* He blinked; the shadowy figures vanished.

An arched doorway opened in front of Pettigrew; it grew in size, and space expanded. A silent pulpit set high under a stone dome drifted past. Pettigrew imagined he saw an old man in white vestments standing behind it. Dim light outlined him. He wore an arched hat and held a golden chalice. He smiled at Pettigrew. Rainbows of light slanted through tall windows and splashed on archways and cornices. The barrel-vaulted ceiling was lost in the dark, high above him. All was still; nothing moved. Pettigrew drew a silent breath.

The silence of centuries is heavy in this place.

"Here we are," said Lawrence.

They clustered in an arch. The rough stones pressed against Pettigrew. His stomach tightened.

"We will wait here."

"I thought I heard a bird chirp," said Pettigrew.

"Be quiet."

Pettigrew held his breath. His heart thumped. He smelled acrid sweat.

"Listen. There it is again."

In the dim, Flinders cocked his head. "You are right."

"I think that we are about to have some action."

A whisper. "Do not move."

The bird chirped again.

Pettigrew felt for his pistol. His hand shook. His fingers closed on the dagger instead. Its handle was slippery.

I am afraid.

"Wait," Lawrence whispered in his ear.

The light faded to orange and cast long shadows of the figures outlined in the windows. Priest and knights moved in the glass; their shapes grew taller as the sun moved behind them.

The windows are alive.

The outlines spread and wavered on the dim floor.

I see hazy shapes rising before me. The orange light swirls through them. Their eyes stare at me.

Pettigrew sensed a furtive movement. Another chirp. A gray shape, barely visible, moved in an archway. He tapped Flinders on the shoulder and pointed.

"I see something."

"Be still."

Pettigrew's hands were slick with sweat.

A voice called out softly from another archway. A second voice answered.

"Wait," Lawrence whispered again. His breath was warm on Pettigrew's ear.

"Someone is here."

"Don't move."

The two shapes met in the middle of the great hall. Pettigrew could barely make them out. One was a tall figure, heavily built, a giant of a man; the other was much smaller and slighter. The smaller figure held out a package.

"Now!"

Pettigrew charged forward. The blade leaped before him. He sensed Flinders at his side. Pistol fire ricocheted off the walls. Doorways flashed out of the blackness and vanished. Figures in the stained glass windows danced in the flares.

They closed the distance. The smaller man raised a knife; its curve was a flickering tongue lit by sudden bursts in the dim light. More flashes. The small man staggered and fell back; his body and arms elongated like a scarecrow blown in a wind. Then he crumpled and disappeared.

"Get him!"

"Get him."

The giant loomed over Pettigrew, his shape checkered with moving light. A distorted smile and two wide, staring eyes framed by unkempt hair swelled across his vision. The eyes glared at Pettigrew. The mouth opened to a blackness. The face ballooned to an enormous moon. Acrid breath engulfed Pettigrew. An arm swung the shadow of a sword; orange light streamed down its edge. The blades clashed. Pettigrew's wrist gave way; his shoulder felt out of joint. Pain seared up and down his arm. The dagger skittered to the stone floor. A hammer blow crushed his chest.

Flashes of light and peels of thunder surrounded him. The rose windows grew to titanic heights. Knights drummed on their shields. Red crosses floated in front of him. Sour incense smothered him. A giant pipe organ droned an off-key hymn. The pulpit's dome blazed in sudden light. The old man in white robes stood and smiled. He rose and drifted down from the altar and floated in front of Pettigrew. He held out the chalice; he wavered and beckoned. His gauzy smile hung in the air. His eyes were kind, but then they turned yellow and glaring. His smile dissolved; his mouth opened. It gaped wider and wider until it became a black emptiness. A pistol fired; the sound split his ear. The world spun sideways and turned from gray to red.

Then, nothing.

"Well now, the hero finally awakes." Flinders's face was upside down, and his brown eyes were wide with concern. "We thought we had lost you. But apparently not."

"What happened?"

"He got away."

Flinders's face disappeared.

"I killed the Hashshashin. The Bulbul Pasha knocked you down. I shot him twice, but it made no difference. Lawrence threw himself at the man, but he bounced off. The Bulbul Pasha grabbed the statue and ran. I shot again and missed him. He dodged through the arches."

Flinders's face reappeared right side up.

"Lawrence tried to tackle him, but he was thrown aside like a rag doll. The Bulbul Pasha had a motorcycle waiting and rode off." Flinders leaned forward. "The Bulbul was clearly too much for us. We were unprepared. The legends do not do him justice. He is far more formidable than we expected."

"You saved my life."

"Nonsense. I merely prevented him from killing you."

"You say he is more formidable."

"Yes."

"And if he is more formidable, what about the Veiled One?"

Flinders shook his head. "I do not know."

"I hurt."

"So you do."

"I feel like a hundred crusaders have pounded on me and ridden their horses over my arm."

"And so they have."

Flinders's face retreated.

"I am not surprised. You took a tremendous blow. Luckily, you parried his blade, and he hit you with the pommel. We put you on Nellie and carried you back to camp. Nellie was worried. *We* were worried. You have been here for three days. Unayza has never left you. She stays by your side with her sisters."

Lawrence's face appeared. There was a large bruise under his eye. "How are you, old chap? We have missed you." Lawrence fingered the bruise. "That was certainly a scrum." He laughed. "You know, if I had a motorcycle, I could have caught him. I think I will buy one someday. I like the speed."

Pettigrew struggled to sit up. "Where am I hurt?" he asked.

"In the chest."

Pettigrew felt gingerly around. "Ouch." He ran his fingers along his collarbone. "My sternum is bruised but not broken." He passed his hands lightly over his ribs. "Nothing displaced, maybe some cracked ribs. But perhaps not. Rest is the only cure."

"We will be here for a few more days."

Pettigrew sat up with difficulty and looked around. He was in a small tent. It was different from the one he remembered. Its floor was covered with colorful carpets and pillows. A small brazier held a low fire. Incense swirled. He touched his chest; it was covered with some sort of poultice.

Where am I?

"Where are you?" Lawrence read his mind. "You are in a tent that Unayza prepared." He chuckled. "Unayza says this medicine is from the time of the prophet. It will heal your broken bones. She has nursed you herself. Now you are doubly honored."

He looked thoughtful. "A bedouin woman takes care of you. She is as hard as the desert and as soft as a rose." He laughed heartily. "But be careful what you do, because you may end up married, with ten strong sons, daughters all over, and a hundred camels."

He leaned over Pettigrew. "Even Imrul Qays himself would not be able to rescue you." He whistled a few bars of "It's a Long Way to Tipperary," lifted the tent flap, and left. "Good night, Abul hol."

Flinders watched him go. "A strange man. Perhaps someday the world will understand him." He shrugged. "But we have another task." He stood up. "While you are recovering, I will make inquiries. I think that we will have to go to Istanbul. I've been in touch with Gertrude. She has gone to Istanbul. She writes that she has contacts. They say that the Veiled One is in hiding there. Get some rest." Flinders left as well.

Pettigrew lay back and dozed off.

When he opened his eyes again, he saw that opal light had flooded the tent. It was morning. Flinders and Lawrence were sitting on ottomans and drinking coffee. Unayza knelt beside him; she was changing the poultice.

Who is this woman who cares for me? Tears clouded his vision. *There was only one other woman that cared for me. And she is dead.*

He reached out and touched Unayza's hand. She smiled.

Lawrence stood up and put his cup down. "You are fortunate—the shaykh has decided to stay here for the rest of the year. He says that water and grass are plentiful, and that his people and animals will grow fat." He laughed. "You must be protected by the prophet himself."

Two more days passed. Pettigrew regained his strength. Every morning, Unayza came into his tent. Often, she brought other women. Pettigrew memorized her movements. He began to long for the feel of her hands as she changed the poultice.

Can I grow so accustomed to a person that her presence becomes part of my very being? I can hear the rhythm of her steps as she enters the tent. The jingle of her bracelets is music to my ears. I can sense her breathing as she bends over me. Her eyes smile at me.

On the morning of the third day, Flinders came into the tent.

"Are you well enough to leave tomorrow?"

"Yes, I think so."

"Then tonight is our last night. The car has returned from Carchemish."

Pettigrew slept most of the day. When he woke, he could see evening shadows moving outside the tent. Talking and laughter burbled in his ears.

Animals coughed. Cooking smells flooded the tent. Its coverings and poles sung a slow rhythm in the desert air. The hum lulled him.

There is a strange peace here in spite of the harshness. Perhaps in another life . . . and he fell back into sleep.

He felt Unayza slip into the blanket. Her body was long beside him. Her hair caressed his face. Her lips were warm. Her perfume washed over him.

"*Habibi, habibi*; beloved, beloved."

His fingers crept down.

My fingers have a life of their own. She is so soft; I cannot stop.

They became one in the silence.

When he woke up, she was gone.

Was this real, or was I dreaming? But what am I to do?

"Yes. What *are* you to do?" said a voice.

He closed his eyes, and his mind wandered.

The light streamed over the cobbles. A door opened. Music and laughter overwhelmed him. She turned. "I dance very well. I will dance with you if you like." He stood there . . .

In the morning, he arose and put on his khakis. He stepped out of the tent. The air was still dark; the sun had not yet crept over the horizon. No one was around; the camp slept. Somewhere a camel groaned.

Flinders was already in the car. "Hurry, we must leave."

Lawrence stood beside the car. "I will stay here. I do not like crowded cities."

The engine growled. Pettigrew got in. The car jerked forward and began to roll. The camp receded behind them. Waves of dust trailed the car. Pettigrew did not look back. For if he did, he felt that he would have to acknowledge something he did not wish to admit.

She is as hard as the desert and as soft as a rose.

SEVEN

What Manner of Men

Pettigrew got up from the bed. The sounds of Istanbul murmured through the closed window. He shook his head at the memories.

I have become the sailor condemned to sail the sea forever.

He went to the mirror and peered at the figure he saw in it. A face with blond hair and twinkly blue eyes looked back. He rubbed the square chin. There was a knock, and then Flinders burst through the door.

"I thought that I heard a crash. You haven't been practicing savate again, have you?" Flinders clapped his hands together briskly. "Get dressed; we are to meet Gertrude at the embassy in an hour. She seems eager to see you." He grinned. "For the life of me, I cannot fathom why."

Pettigrew got dressed. Flinders opened the room door. Hotel sounds flooded in. They went through the lobby and out the ornate front door. Street noises exploded in Pettigrew's ear.

"Come along," Flinders said. "The car is waiting."

The drive was short. The car drove along a waterfront. Domes and fingerlike minarets flowed past. Flags rolled and flapped slowly in the breeze. Gray ships lined the horizon—motionless statues whose shapes were reflected by the dark water. Steamers honked. Gulls circled and screeched. The wind smelled of seawater.

The embassy was a large white building with corners capped by square turrets. A Union Jack flew bravely on a long flagstaff. Flinders studied the building as the car stopped in front of the wide front door.

"Odd architecture. I cannot place it. It looks very ornate with all the cupolas and balconies."

"Now you have become an architect?"

"I am a classical scholar. I once helped Edward Lutyens design country houses." Flinders grinned. "You were busy cutting up frogs in your room."

They got out, and the car pulled away.

A guard in blue ushered them up seemingly endless flights of stairs. The guard opened a door, and Pettigrew saw a room with a table. Portraits of fierce-looking men with medals covered the walls. The floor was bare. Three people sat behind the table: two men and a woman. He recognized Gertrude. A large man in red sat in the center and wore medals. He gestured that they enter.

"Come in. Please close the door behind you."

They sat in wicker chairs. Gertrude was to his right; she had changed from her khakis to a long black dress. Her green eyes searched Pettigrew's face. She smiled. "Ah, Thomas, I heard about your injury. I was worried. But I see that you are well."

He smiled back. "Still a little sore."

"Nothing serious?"

"No."

"Good trip?"

"Yes."

The green eyes continued searching. The smile remained fixed.

"That is good."

"Thank you."

Their eyes met.

She turned to the man in red sitting next to her. "This is Ambassador Lowther."

The man rose and shook their hands. He had a long face and white hair. His eyes smiled.

"Glad to meet you," he said. "Your reputation precedes you."

"And this"—Gertrude gestured at the other man sitting at the end of the table—"is Kudret Bey, our intelligence director."

The man also smiled. He stood and leaned forward; his earrings glistened as he stretched out his hand. He wore a large gold chain and bracelets.

"So, the famous detectives," he said. "I have read about your adventures in Egypt. I am honored." His voice was low; his English was flawless. He sat down and folded his arms across gray lapels.

Pettigrew looked closely at him. He saw a small man in a Western suit. The man was clean-shaven with curls and long black hair. His movements were fluid. "Nice to meet you also."

"Now, let us get to the point." The ambassador steepled his hands. "You are here to recover a statue that has been stolen from the British Museum."

Pettigrew and Flinders both nodded.

"You think that it has been stolen by an individual known as the Veiled One. And you want our assistance in recovering it."

"Precisely so," Flinders agreed.

The ambassador studied a yellow paper and then looked up. "The prime minister has cabled me and ordered me to aid you. It seems that your Director Budge was most persuasive." He shuffled some folders in front of him. "How may we help?"

"We believe that the statue may be here in Istanbul," Flinders said quietly, "and that it is in the possession of the Veiled One. We would like your help in finding its location." Flinders smiled. "We will do the rest."

"Kudret, what do you think?" Lowther turned to the other man.

"It will not be easy." Kudret rubbed his chin. "The Veiled One is very clever. We have only sketchy knowledge of his whereabouts."

Kudret put his elbows on the table. "He moves like a jinn."

The jinn again.

The ambassador leaned forward and repeated himself. "How can we help?"

"If you could find us some leads," Flinders said, "we can proceed from there."

"Do you speak Turkish?" Kudret interrupted. When they shook their heads no, he said, "I thought not."

Kudret pulled at an earring. "We will handle the investigation. Remember, 'two captains sink the ship.' Even Ottoman intelligence has been unable to locate the Veiled One." Kudret fingered his chain. "And Ottoman intelligence is very good—they can even read your king's mail before he does." He smiled. "However, we are better. We read their mail even before they read the king's."

Gertrude laughed; the ambassador chuckled.

"We have tried to find him many times without success." Kudret sat back. "But remember, 'a defeated wrestler is not tired of wrestling.' I think that I can find him."

Gertrude interrupted. "Don't you already have an extensive dossier?"

"Yes, but not as complete as I would like. Let me summarize it for you." Kudret put on a pair of rimless spectacles and opened a thick file lined with red stripes. "The Veiled One was the son of an ancient family. His father was a general who commanded Ottoman troops in the Crimea. They withstood the Russians in Silistra but then collapsed at the siege of Sinop. The sultan was enraged; he had given the general lands and gifts for his bravery."

He stopped reading. "I knew the general. A fine man." He smiled. "The general once passed by my village. He saw me and called out, 'Kudret, what are you doing here? You should be back in Istanbul.' I was very young and had just been taken into the palace.

"Yes," Kudret said, smiling at the memory, "a fine man. But to continue . . . the sultan ordered the general to be punished. The general's lands were seized, his houses were burned, and his family was executed. The young man was forced to watch his father, mother, and sisters impaled. They screamed and died horribly."

"They were impaled?" Flinders frowned.

Kudret turned a page. "The young man was taken to Istanbul and sentenced to be burned alive. But the flames burned the ropes that bound him, and he escaped. He murdered two men and swore to kill the sultan."

"Brutal. All of it."

"Yes. He was horribly burned in the fire. It is said that he had no skin on his face, only bones and eye sockets. He has worn a silver veil ever since."

"A disfigured monster." Pettigrew grimaced.

He became a jinn.

"Yes."

"And what about the Bulbul?"

"We don't know much about him." Kudret reached for another file. "He appeared out of nowhere and became the Veiled One's second in command." He opened the file and frowned. "There is not much here. His name says it all. A bulbul is a nightingale, a bird that sings as dusk turns into night. The state executioner's official title is Bulbul Pasha. I'm sure that you can grasp the connection. He is a giant of a man, and his face is a mask of hate."

"We have met him."

"So I heard." Kudret nodded. "Do not be embarrassed; he killed two of my strongest men.

"I will tell you a tale," Kudret said. "We thought we had him cornered in the catacombs beneath the Hagia Sophia. He dodged us down the cistern's steps and disappeared among the columns. We waded through the water, trying to be as quiet as possible. There was no sound except the trickle of water. Our torches reflected off the walls. Columns and shadows of columns danced before our eyes. There was nothing but silence."

Kudret leaned forward on his elbows.

"Nothing but silence and water dripping. Then came a roar." Kudret opened his eyes wide. "The roar reverberated off the columns." His spectacles glinted. "The Bulbul was behind us. He knocked me into the water. He picked Mehmet and Aydar up and smashed their heads together."

Kudret frowned. "Then he laughed and threw their bodies at us. The splash covered our eyes. We were blinded. When we could see again, he was gone."

Kudret leaned back in his seat. "Mehmet and Aydar were my friends. I had to tell their wives." He took off the spectacles; the lenses were fogged. "You were lucky, effendis."

"We look forward to a second meeting," Pettigrew said.

"You English are insouciant," Kudret said with a laugh. "There is a proverb that describes you: 'A man is harder than iron, stronger than stone, and more fragile than a rose.' Be careful what you seek." He closed the file. "I think that I can find someone who can tell us more about him."

"And the statue?" Pettigrew asked. "What about the statue?"

"The statue of Aphrodite had been in the Veiled One's family for generations. It was his mother's favorite piece. She kept it on a small stand in her bedroom. As she died screaming on the stake, the Ottoman soldiers played catch with it in front of her. The sultan later gave it to the officer in command along with all the family's lands."

"That explains why the Veiled One would want it back," Pettigrew said.

"It explains quite a lot," Kudret said. He leaned back in his chair.

"I can see why the general sold it to the museum."

"He was in fear for his life."

"The Veiled One will not give it up easily," Pettigrew concluded.

Kudret frowned. "That is the best that I can give you at present." He folded his arms. "I will make inquiries. It will take a few days." He smiled. "Remember, 'patience is the key to paradise.'"

Gertrude said, "We will contact you in a day or so."

"I take it that you are at the Pera Palace Hotel?" Kudret grinned. "An excellent hotel. Enjoy the nightlife while you wait."

Everyone got up and left the room, the guards closing the door after them. They descended the stairs. On the way down, Pettigrew asked Gertrude, "Who is this Kudret?"

She paused, her hand on the oak banister. "Kudret is the head of intelligence here. He is a kocek."

"Kocek?"

"Yes, a kocek . . . a male belly dancer."

"A male belly dancer?"

She took several steps and turned to look at him. "You do not understand. Koceks are young men who have been trained to dance since childhood. They learn all the arts of seduction."

"Seduction?"

"Yes."

"Indeed."

"They are honored here." She stepped onto the landing.

"Honored?"

"Yes, they are an old tradition, and Kudret is the perfect agent."

"A tradition?"

She paused. "The Ottoman Empire has existed for one thousand years. It has many traditions." She walked toward the door. "Women do not dance in front of men. Male dancers perform. The Ottoman elite watch only male dancers. They sit around in private houses in small groups—officials, generals, and police." She grinned. "Even the sultan's family members."

Gertrude's green eyes danced. "They smoke and drink and lust. They talk, and Kudret listens." She smiled. "He has female dancers as well; his dancers, male or female, are welcome in the harems of the officials. No one notices his dancers. He has infiltrated the entire Ottoman government." Her eyes became mischievous. "Who would have thought the stodgy English would do such a thing?"

Flinders frowned. "A network of male dancers? And what else?"

"This is not England."

"I see. But . . ."

"You must understand, this is the way things are done here. And Kudret is the best." She opened the embassy door. "He has a direct line to Ottoman intelligence. Anything the Ottomans know about the Veiled One, he can find out." She held the door open. "You will see."

Flinders shot a quizzical glance at Gertrude. "Has he . . . ?"

"I do not know. He does not have a beard."

Flinders lifted an eyebrow.

She shrugged. "Sometimes. When the information needed is particularly valuable."

Pettigrew listened. *There is more to Gertrude than I thought.*

He stepped out and turned to face her. "We will be in touch," he said.

Flinders made his way toward the car.

Gertrude's eyes fixed on Pettigrew. "Goodbye for now."

"Goodbye."

The door closed. The car drove slowly back to the hotel. Troops of gray-clad cavalry, harnesses and bits clinking, trotted past. The car pushed its way through crowds of pedestrians. Men and women wearing caps and turbans bustled by.

"Their hats are fantastic," Flinders said. In front of them, two men greeted each other. The exchange was long and accompanied by elaborate bowing and hand movements.

"Curious," said Pettigrew. "Gertrude told me about Ottoman etiquette. She said that it was almost impossible to end a conversation, and that you had to say *izninizle*—'with your permission'—at least three times before you could withdraw. She explained that social relations here are more important than business." Her eyes had flashed as they talked.

"You know a lot about the Middle East," he had told her.

"Remember, I grew up traveling the Levant," she had said.

"And you have never stopped," he had said.

"No. And I never will." She laughed.

The car stopped to let a squad of marching men past. They had rifles on their shoulders. Pedestrians and push carts scattered out of their way.

"Curious, you say." Flinders leaned forward and watched the troopers go. "Maybe so. But maybe they have a politeness that we have lost. Tall hats, short hats, hats shaped like onions, hats shaped like cones . . . turbans three feet across." Flinders grinned. "It is a haberdasher's paradise."

"I asked Gertrude about the hats," Pettigrew replied. "She said, 'Headgear marks rank and position here.'" Pettigrew smiled. "We wear rank on our shoulders and sleeves. They wear rank and position on their heads. She said that each rank has a formal way of address and the language has many ways of expressing them."

Meeting her again was strange. "They call me the Queen of the Desert," she had once told me, her tone conspiratorial. Her eyes twinkled. "Do you think that I am a queen, Mr. Pettigrew?"

"I thought that Lady Hester was queen of the desert."

The green eyes had danced. "A beginner." She looked at me and laughed. "I know more about the desert and the sown than she will ever know. But some things remain a mystery to me." The green eyes became very serious.

The car started again. A young boy tried to reach through the window to hand Pettigrew a bunch of tulips. Pettigrew pushed them away.

"You should buy the flowers," Flinders said.

Gertrude had shown me into her temporary office before we left the embassy. She had a vase of tulips on her desk. "Tulips are the mark of a great civilization." She came close to me. "Tulips are also the sign of love."

"Flowery greetings." Flinders sat back in his seat. "Our English does not use them. Do you suppose that we are missing something?" He watched the hats flow by the car. "Some of them are astonishingly large—I wonder how they can balance them."

"A queen," she had said. Yes, you are a queen, but I don't know what to do about you.

Pettigrew laughed. "But you should wonder how Englishmen balance all those medals and sashes that we wear." He turned from the car window. "Do you remember the Queen's diamond jubilee? There were enough hats, sashes, and medals for three Ottoman empires."

Or how to feel about you.

Flinders laughed. "You are right; we have strange customs too." His eyes twinkled. "Thomas, do you suppose that we have come to the horizon beyond the horizon?"

The horizon beyond the horizon. But is the horizon without, or is it within?

"This is a strange place." Pettigrew laughed. "But you look very natural here."

"Strange, indeed."

"But wonderful."

"Wonderful?" Flinders arched an eyebrow. "Whatever happened to 'I don't want to be a pasha'?" He grinned. "I believe that was what you said in Cairo."

"People change," Pettigrew growled.

The car stopped in front of the hotel door.

The dinner was excellent. They had a drink in the bar.

"This reminds me of the bar at the Shepard's in Cairo." Flinders examined the room with approval. "Now all we need is an orchestra and some ladies."

"So you could dance tango, I suppose?"

"The ladies were most enthusiastic." Flinders smiled at the memory.

"I think I will go to bed." Pettigrew yawned.

"It's too early; you are truly becoming an old maid."

"It's been a long day."

"What, no belly dancers?"

"Maybe not tonight. Let me think about it."

There was a belly dancer in Cairo. She whirled in front of me. Sami laughed. "Are you man enough to tip her? Just put this pound note between your fingers. When she comes to you, stuff it in her girdle. I will order some arak."

They retired to their rooms. An hour later, Flinders pounded on the door. "Well, do you want to see some belly dancing? After all, we are in Istanbul."

Pettigrew grimaced. "I think I will stay in my room."

"Nonsense. You need to get out."

"I do not want to see belly dancing—I had quite enough of it in Cairo."

"You will have to change your tastes. Broaden them, you might say." Flinders pushed Pettigrew back into his room. "Come, let us get dressed."

Pettigrew put on a suit and tied his tie.

I wore a dark suit then. The Schaherazade Club was crowded. We sat at a table; Sami sat across from me. Our eyes met. "I will drink to you," she said. She lifted her glass in a toast and drank. Her eyes opened wide in surprise.

He turned to face Flinders. "Well?"

Flinders examined him with disapproval. "Thomas, you could never learn to tie a decent cravat. Let me fix it."

He tied my cravat the night we went to the Schaherazade.

He did so and then studied himself in the mirror. "It is the couture that makes the man." He smoothed his hair.

"Kudret will meet us. He has given me the address of a tavern on Galata Street." He smiled. "The concierge said that it is known as 'the street of the women.'"

And so they went.

The car dropped them off at the entrance to a narrow street. Pettigrew looked down its narrow and twisted length. Its cobbles were broken and worn. Latticed porches dappled the light. Donkeys passed. Venders called and shouted. The street smelled of sweat and alcohol. They walked and dodged occasional piles of dung. A boy selling tulips blocked their way. Pettigrew protested—they really didn't need tulips—but Flinders bought a bunch. He smiled and held the flowers out to Pettigrew. "Tulips are the rage here."

A passerby bumped Pettigrew. Pettigrew searched his pockets, but nothing seemed to be missing. Rows of women sat on wooden chairs along their path. A few wore no clothes. They pouted and called out. Men, some in suits and fezzes, some in striped kaftans, jackets, and turbans, bargained with them. Women leered and gestured as they passed. One or two ran into the street and tugged at their sleeves. Flinders smiled and gently shook them off. "Not today, I think."

Two boys in long dresses, with curly hair, makeup, and necklaces, giggled and wiggled.

"Those are boys," Pettigrew growled. He pulled his fedora down. "I think we are in the heart of debauchery."

Flinders nodded. "Indeed, that seems the case."

Kudret met them at the tavern's entrance. A wooden door led to a flight of narrow stairs. The room was small and hot. Tobacco smoke clouded Pettigrew's vision and filled his nose. Men sat around the tables that lined the walls. They talked and laughed, puffs of smoke condensing in the steamy air above them. Waiters in kaftans and fezzes carried trays loaded with drinks and food. Glasses clinked noisily; silverware scratched on plates.

"You have seen belly dancing before?" Kudret asked.

"Yes, in Cairo."

"Our dancing is much quicker and more exciting than you saw there. The Egyptians are slow and boring."

A waiter brought small glasses of a colorless liquid and set the bottle on the table.

"This is raki."

Flinders took a sip. Pettigrew followed.

"It tastes like licorice," Flinders said.

"It tastes like arak," Pettigrew added.

I held her in my arms. Her arms and legs flailed. She bit her lips. I could smell the arsenic. Flinders bent over us. His face was shocked. "There is no antidote for arsenic," I said.

Kudret grinned. "Be careful—it is deceptive. It is like a young maiden who smiles at you in front, and then her brother beats you from behind and takes your money."

They drank.

"I see that you have bought some tulips," Kudret said, gesturing to the bunch of flowers Flinders had tossed on the table. "Do you have tulips in England?"

"Yes. They are much admired there."

"I always keep a fresh bunch in my divan. Our tulips are famous. A century ago, everyone here grew tulips. We call it the Tulip Era. It was a time of peace and prosperity." He took the tulips. "Remember, 'to give a tulip is to give peace.'" He drained his glass. "We were great, once." Kudret stroked his chin. "Yes, very great. But now there is a war coming, and we shall not survive." He signaled the waiter. "Raki medicates, but it does not cure."

But arak kills. I was a physician, but I could not save her. I held her until the convulsions ended. Her breath stopped. Her head lolled in my arms.

"We must leave at once," Flinders said. "That poison was meant for us."

The dancers came on.

Kudret lit a cigarette, leaned back, and blew a smoke ring. His earrings flashed. "Now you will see something."

A line of young men was strung across the bare floor—figures dressed in all red. They wore caps, long pants, and wide skirts. Beads gleamed and curls fluttered. A small orchestra beat the music. Drums throbbed and castanets clicked.

"They look very young, almost like children," Flinders remarked.

"They are supposed to look young—they wear makeup to enhance that appearance."

The dancers whirled around the room. Skirts billowed; scarves floated. The boys pouted and flirted. Men got up and tried to hug them, staggering awkwardly. Their glasses sloshed and spilled; their cigarettes fell. They pushed one another. The boys laughed and pointed and easily avoided them.

"They act like women. But they are men dressed as women."

"Yes, effendi."

"I don't understand."

"Women do not dance in public here."

Flinders swirled his raki. "I understand that you recruit dancers."

"I do."

"Are any of these yours?"

"Of course, but I cannot tell you who." Kudret put his finger across his lips. "I cannot reveal my agents. They are everywhere."

"The one on the end, I think. The blond."

"The Circassian? No. He probably works for Ottoman intelligence." Kudret whispered, "The sultan has spies everywhere. And where they go, we go too."

"Curious," Pettigrew said, joining the conversation. "Why Circassians? I thought they were a tribe from the Caucasus."

"They are, but they are alien to the Muslim population." He smiled. "You Englishmen are so new, effendi. You do not understand the politics of demography. The Ottomans brought them in because they could be trusted. They have no blood ties with the Muslims."

"But now you say that Circassians dominate Ottoman intelligence."

"That is the price for loyalty."

"Your empire is strange to us," Pettigrew said.

"You are a young people. We were old before there ever was an England." He thumped his glass on the table. "We are the heirs to the Roman Empire. You have seen the tulips, effendi. Tulips are us—a flower that forever changes colors." He put his glass down. "We are forever changing colors."

"But your intelligence . . ."

"There is a saying: 'We need the shadow to see the sun.' Ottoman intelligence is the best in the world." He laughed. "Except for us, of course." He poured more raki into his glass. "I should not drink, but I think that I am with friends. It is well said, 'A good friend is shown on a black day.'"

Pettigrew held out his glass. "I'll drink to that."

"I am tired, friends. Forgive me." Kudret swirled the raki. "My era is passing, along with the tulips."

"How did you come to be director of intelligence?"

Kudret fingered his glass and thought for a moment. He took another drink. He flicked an ash. He leaned forward. His eyes searched the ceiling. "All right, I will tell you."

His voice was low. "When I was a boy, my parents sold me. They were poor and had many mouths to feed and had no choice." He took another sip. "I was taken to the sultan's palace. There were many boys, and some were very young. I was taught to dance and to wiggle my hips, to be seductive to men. We danced in harems and private houses."

He put the glass down. "Men fondled me. Then they wanted more."

The detectives looked at each other.

"I became a well-known dancer." Kudret smiled wistfully, and then his face went dark. "I was invited everywhere. Then, one morning, two men came to see me." He took a long drink. "They were ugly. They said, 'We want you to work for us. Tell us everything you hear.'" He stared into the empty glass. "One of them smiled at me and said, 'If you don't, we know where your family lives.'" He reached for the bottle. "I reported on many people. Many of them disappeared. Their families grieved."

He drew a ring on the table with the raki bottle. "'You harvest what you sow.' I will never be clean." He looked up. "What else do you want to know, effendi?"

"Do you still dance?"

"No. I am too old. And besides, I am now an intelligence director." Kudret drained his glass and grinned. "The English approached me and offered a handsome living."

He chuckled. "Your Gertrude was most persuasive." He poured another glass. "She said, 'We will protect your family.'" He laughed. "So I changed sides. It was luck, pure luck. But remember, 'a man does not seek his luck—luck seeks its man.'"

"You speak English perfectly."

"I know many languages. A spy must listen to many tongues."

"Many tongues?"

"The empire speaks with a thousand voices." His eyes clouded. "This is a great empire—it has many people and many languages. It has lasted for one thousand years. But it is coming to an end. I can feel it." He sighed. "Soon, the empire will be no more. What a loss."

Kudret took a long drink and put his head in his hands. "What a loss," he repeated. He looked up. "You Englishmen do not understand. You call us the 'Sick Men of Europe.' You call us 'backward.' You laugh at our traditions." The glass banged on the table. "But while you were squabbling in medieval darkness, we held the candle of civilization."

The raki left spots on the table. He peered into his glass. "I am sorry. I drink too much these days. Please forget what I said."

Pettigrew took a sip. "Your words have no echo."

"Spoken like an imam, effendi." He laughed. "As I said, 'A good friend is shown on a black day.'"

The dancers left the floor through a small door. Men blew kisses and puckered their lips. Others tried to follow the boys; men struggled with one another to get at the dancers. They started yelling.

Pettigrew looked at Kudret.

"You don't want to know what they are saying," Kudret said as he lit another cigarette. Some men slipped and fell. Hats and shoes littered the floor; liquor puddled across it. Stench covered the room. Waiters blocked the door.

"Do fights always happen?"

"Often. Drunken men cannot control their lust."

"Indeed."

"Would you like to meet them?"

Flinders looked at Pettigrew and then nodded.

Kudret stood up. "Follow me."

He led them to an arched doorway covered with a curtain. A hall opened onto a small room. It smelled of perfume. The dancers were changing out of their costumes. They laughed and shouted. Caps fluttered; chains jingled. They greeted Kudret with shouts and gathered around him; he laughed and hugged them.

"They are all young boys," Pettigrew said.

"Yes."

"Some are very young."

"Yes. Yes, some will grow beards and go back to their villages. Others will stay and dance." He gestured at a tall boy sitting on a bench. He sat alone. The noise swirled around him. "That is Osman. He is Romani. They are old people. The Romani have been wandering the earth for centuries."

I have seen their wagons with their bright yellow wheels in England. Our car has bright yellow wheels. Do we wander together?

"Osman is from my village. He can tell you his story. I will translate."

He spoke to the boy. The boy answered. He looked down.

"Listen to what he tells you."

"When I was very young," the boy began, "I was taken from my village and carried to a camp. There were many boys there." He took off his cap. "I missed my mother and father and brothers. I was taught to dance. Men beat me when I did not learn fast enough."

He opened his jacket. "We lived all together in one room and practiced for many months. Then, one night we were taken to a field. It was dark, and I could not see; I stumbled as they pushed me along. Small fires lined the field. Men sat by the fires."

He shivered. "I was cold."

Chatter swirled. Clothes littered the floor. Boys laughed and pummeled one another.

Osman unbuttoned his shirt. "There were lines of boys and small camels. I asked the man, 'What was this?'"

He took off the shirt and threw it down. His face darkened.

"The man said, 'This is the night of the young camels.'"

"'The young camels?' I asked. 'What does that mean?'"

"'You will see soon enough.'"

Boys threw clothes around; some hit Osman, but he did not move.

He looked at Kudret. "I was afraid. The camels were led out. They walked in a line like a caravan. Their eyes were wide with fear. Men prodded them with sticks. Men with shears waited; they cut the camels. The camels screamed and ran. Some fell and kicked their legs. Men with hammers came to them."

He wiped his nose. "The field smelled of smoke and blood."

He sat down and bent over. He covered his face with his hands.

Kudret patted him on the shoulder and looked at Flinders and Pettigrew. "Do you want to hear more?"

"Yes."

The boys laughed and threw more clothes.

"Then the boys were led out. A long line of boys passed me and walked toward the fires. I could see their shapes outlined by the fire and smoke. Their shadows slanted across the field in front of them. Men marched alongside them; they laughed and pushed the boys along. Some tried to run away. They cried and were afraid. Then the men threw them down. They screamed in pain. The screams echoed across the field."

He dodged a shoe.

"Two men seized my arms."

He rolled up his clothes.

"They threw me down and held me."

He stared at Kudret; his eyes were wide.

"The shears were cold."

"Come on, let's go home," a tall boy yelled. "Dinner is waiting."

Boys tumbled toward the door. Osman folded his jacket. His eyes were wet.

"Have you heard enough, effendis?" Kudret hugged the boy and wiped a tear. "Now we must go."

They climbed the stairs and walked into the night. A crescent moon turned the street into silver and black shadows. The chairs were empty of women; the men were gone. The street still smelled of alcohol and sweat. A stray dog ran by them. At the mouth of the street, Kudret hailed a cab.

"Go, please—I will wait here a moment."

The cab drove off. Pettigrew looked back through the small rear window. Kudret stood in the circle of light from a lamppost, and a soft drizzle slanted down. The light outlined his long coat. His head was bent; both hands covered his eyes. The still figure faded into the distance as the cab continued to move. Finally, Pettigrew could see only a faint glow of pale light at the end of a dark corridor. Steamers hooted. The sound was mournful in the fog.

The cab stopped in the mist.

The Pera Palace gleamed with light. Gray streamers swirled around the columns that guarded its entrance. The doorman in his white kaftan greeted them with a flourish. They passed through the lobby and went into the grand salon. Dark red drapes framed its two-story windows, and the stained-glass skylights looked down on them.

Pettigrew sat on one of the red velvet chairs that lined the perimeter of the room. He leaned back, stretched his legs, and rubbed his eyes. "This is a strange place, Flinders." He signaled to a waiter. "Who are these men who do such things?"

Flinders just stared at the velvet wall. In the dining room, a string orchestra started playing a Straus waltz. The music drifted into the salon.

"Roses from the South."

Pettigrew shook his head. "Beautiful music and horrible brutality."

What manner of men live here? I wonder.

"Flinders, you look as though you are about to fall asleep. We must be fresh in the morning." Pettigrew stood. "Good night."

Flinders sat still. "I think I shall stay up a bit longer. The image of the boys haunts me, and this hotel reminds me of Cairo."

He took a glass from the waiter. "Thomas, the look in Osman's eyes was heart-rending. It shook me to the core; old memories came bubbling up." He looked up. His face was suddenly old, and his eyes were haunted. "Thomas, remember when we left the tomb? Inji sang a lullaby. I can still hear that lullaby."

You can still hear the lullaby. I can still hear the laughter and then the screams. The past will never leave us in peace.

Pettigrew walked toward the grand staircase and then turned to look. Flinders sat with his head resting on his elbows.

He is remembering the past.

Pettigrew climbed a few stairs and turned back again, his hand on the marble banister. Flinders had not moved; he was a still, dark figure against the velvet opulence.

We are both haunted by what happened in Egypt.

Pettigrew turned and climbed the stairs; the marble was cold under his hand.

And now we are haunted by what happens here.

He unlocked the room door, climbed into the bed, and went to sleep.

He slept fitfully—dreams of boys crying and camels screaming kept waking him.

What kind of a place is this? Such beauty and such barbarity. Do beauty and barbarity go together?

Then he dozed off again. The bed was hard, and the honks of steamers carried through the window.

EIGHT

The Universe Turns Left

In the morning, tired and hung over, they returned to the embassy. They were sent upstairs to the same room. Four guards accompanied them; two remained outside the door, and two came inside. They stood with their backs to the door and their hands on the hilts of their sabers.

Kudret and Gertrude sat at the table. A stenographer ruffled papers from her small chair. A typewriter on a wheeled stand was in front of her. In a far corner, a vase of tulips wilted listlessly.

Kudret greeted them, grinned, and then said, "You look a little worse for wear. Perhaps the raki agreed with you too much." He looked at Pettigrew. Pettigrew managed a half-hearted nod.

Gertrude chuckled. "How nice to see you this morning," she said. Her eyes flashed. "I can see that you had an interesting evening."

"It was great entertainment; you should have come along."

"Yes, it was marvelous," Flinders chimed in. "Simply marvelous."

"Ah, Mr. Petrie." Gertrude looked concerned. "You appear a little green this morning."

Gertrude, you really are becoming a witch.

The guards rattled their sabers and stared at the ceiling.

"I am quite well, thank you."

"Perhaps the hair of the dog that bit you." Gertrude smiled gently. "I have it! We have some gin downstairs." She looked concerned. "Yes, I'm told that is just the thing. What do you think, Kudret?"

Gertrude, I think I am going to learn to hate you.

"I'm told that fine gentlemen in England drink something called a Singapore Sling before breakfast," Kudret said. "They say it soothes the heart."

Flinders blanched.

And that includes you also, Kudret.

Gertrude blew a smoke ring and watched it dissolve in the air.

"Too sweet, I think." She blew another smoke ring. "Besides, it will dull the alertness. Detectives must always be alert. The great Sherlock Holmes was always alert." She swung her chair around. "Don't you agree, Mr. Pettigrew?"

"But of course."

Gertrude, you are becoming evil before my eyes.

"Possibly garlic," Gertrude said and produced a dazzling smile. "Mr. Pettigrew, would you like some garlic in your gin?"

Flinders shivered.

The stenographer held some papers to her face.

Gertrude, I think that I may want to strangle you.

"Good idea!" Kudret clapped his hands. "The ambassador always has a glass of gin and garlic in the morning."

Th stenographer coughed behind her paper.

"Lale, are you all right?"

"Just some dust, sir."

"Of course." Kudret smiled.

"I didn't know the ambassador drank gin with garlic." Gertrude feigned surprise.

"Oh, yes." Kudret's face was earnest. "He has his gin along with toast and strawberry jam. He said it made him the man he is."

"The man is a troll," Flinders muttered to himself.

One more word from either of you . . .

"Perhaps you would like some of the same, Mr. Pettigrew." Gertrude's eyes were bottomless green pools.

"Just coffee, please."

Strangling may be too good . . .

"Of course." Gertrude's eyes were wicked. "Let me pour you a cup. I am sure that will help."

She smiled at Flinders. "Some coffee for you as well?"

"Yes, thank you." Flinders looked relieved.

The coffee was strong and hot. After several cups, Pettigrew looked around. The tulips stood at attention and smiled brightly at him.

Kudret picked up a file and opened it. "We have found a witness. Someone who can tell us about the Bulbul. Lale here has just finished typing his dossier." He nodded to the stenographer, and the stenographer smiled back. "He is an old man who once lived in the Bulbul's village."

Lale folded her equipment and rolled the typewriter out of the room.

Kudret continued, "He is willing to meet us at a coffeehouse. It is a dangerous location, and there may be spies. The Ottoman government watches everybody. We must be careful."

"Difficult," Flinders said, "but I think that we can manage it."

Kudret smiled. "Do you know how to play backgammon? They play backgammon in these places, and we will too."

"I do." Flinders grinned. "I was a backgammon champion at Oxford."

"We will see about that." Kudret handed them fezzes. "So you will look like Ottoman gentlemen."

Gertrude stood at the embassy door and watched them leave. Her lips smiled, but her eyes were worried.

They got in the car and drove along tree-lined avenues. Onion-topped mosques with tall minarets flowed by. Pedestrians and animals slid past them. Venders shouted; carts rumbled; animals complained. A troupe of men in tall conical hats and flowing white robes walked ahead of them. Pettigrew watched them through the windscreen.

"They are Sufis," Kudret said. "They commune with God by whirling until they go into a trance. You Englishmen call them whirling dervishes."

The car pulled abreast of the men, and Pettigrew rolled down the window. "They wear white."

"The white robes symbolize their surrender to God, effendi. It is the color of their shrouds."

"Shrouds?"

"Yes, effendi, shrouds for death of their selfishness." Kudret laughed. "Are you English capable of rejecting your selfishness?"

Pettigrew leaned out the window. "They are chanting."

"They are reciting their prayers," Kudret said. "They are going to a zikr, a religious meeting. When they arrive, they will pray and begin turning left until they see the face of God."

"Turning left?"

"That is the way the universe turns, effendi."

Pettigrew shrugged.

"If you turn left long enough, you will see the face of God."

"No one sees the face of God."

"These men do," Kudret said with a laugh. "You English have forgotten your piety."

Will I ever see the face of God?

Pettigrew twisted and stared as the men in white receded behind the car. The car turned into a narrow lane and stopped. In front of them was a building with arched windows. Moisture clouded the windows. Its doors were open.

"We are here."

Pettigrew smelled roasting coffee. They got out and entered. The coffeehouse was almost empty. The tiled floor was covered in carpets. A line of tables ran around the walls. A few men in fezzes and turbans sat at them. Brass braziers rested on copper trays. Waiters lounged behind low counters. Coffee steamed; tobacco smoke drifted. Water pipes bubbled.

"No one comes here at this time of day."

An old man was sitting alone at the far end. He wore a brown gallabi-yah and a white skull cap. He smoked a water pipe, and there was a glass of tea on the table.

Kudret pointed. "He is the one."

They pulled out chairs and sat down. Chair legs scraped on the tile.

"Tunayden, good afternoon." Kudret bowed to the old man. "We have come to listen to your story, bilge baba, wise father." He gestured. "I will translate."

A waiter brought small cups of coffee.

"You will find it very strong," Kudret said. He produced a backgammon board and set up the pieces. He handed the dice to Flinders. "Now, Englishman, let me see your skill."

Both men bent over the board. Pettigrew sipped the coffee and watched.

Kudret handed the dice cup to Flinders. "You may go first, Englishman." Then he spoke to the old man. "Please tell us what you know, wise father."

Flinders rolled the dice.

The old man pulled at his beard and began. "Yes, I know who the Bulbul is. He came from my village." He lifted his glass and swirled the tea.

Flinders moved a piece.

"Go on, please."

"It was a long time ago." He studied the tea and then put the glass down. "There was a boy."

"A boy?"

Flinders handed the dice cup to Kudret.

The old man nodded. His eyes were watery. "I knew the boy. He was a big boy but very quiet. He had an old white dog. The boy called the dog Abdu. He would scratch the dog's ears, and the dog would lick the boy's face. Every morning for years, the boy and the dog would go to the mosque. The dog would wait outside."

A waiter brought more coffee. The coffeehouse became more crowded. Men in fezzes ordered coffee in loud voices. Waiters whisked between tables. Steam droplets covered the windows. Pipe smoke layered the room.

"The boy would go in and help the imam clean the mosque. As he grew older and taller, he and the imam would study together. The boy wanted to become an imam himself. The imam was blind, and the boy would lead him around."

He drew a long puff from the pipe. The water gurgled.

Kudret shook the dice and moved a piece.

"After the lessons, the boy and the dog would sit in the sun outside the mosque and study. This went on for years. The boy grew to be a giant. As the imam grew older and feebler, the boy would carry him around on his back."

Pettigrew closed his eyes for a moment and imagined the scene.

The boy sits with his dog; the sun warms them both. The dog cocks its head and listens while the boy reads the Koran. The boy scratches the dog behind its ears. Then the boy, now a giant, goes into the mosque. The dog sits in the sun and waits.

"Aha! Take that!" Flinders slammed a piece on the board, and Pettigrew's eyes flew open.

Kudret frowned.

The old man drank some tea; the glass shook in his hands. Some tea spilled. He looked at the glass and sighed. His hands were gnarled and discolored.

Kudret looked at the board and folded his arms. "Can you go on, father?"

Flinders picked up the dice cup.

Dice clicked.

"Then, late one day, a troop of Cossacks entered the village. They were looking for Armenians. They were drunk and did not care what they did. They entered the mosque and started breaking things. They dragged the old imam outside and handed him a sword. 'Defend your mosque,' they said."

The old man covered his face.

The players stopped. The cups stilled. The dice were silent.

"The imam swung the sword, but he could not see. He cried and wailed. They formed a circle around him and slowly cut him to pieces."

Pettigrew closed his eyes again.

He staggered and swung in the dark. He could hear laughs coming from nowhere. He winced at the sudden cuts. He smelled his own blood.

Pettigrew could hear Flinders taking a deep breath. The sound seemed very far away.

Bubbles rose and burst in the pipe's bowl.

Pettigrew did not move. His mind took over.

He fell on the dusty earth outside the mosque floor. His blood stained the ground. He twitched and then lay motionless.

Kudret set up the board again. "You were lucky, Englishman." He turned to their storyteller. "Do you want to rest?" he asked gently.

The old man shook his head.

Kudret signaled a waiter and ordered more coffee.

The old man's voice quavered. The twisted fingers tapped the table. "They tied the boy up. They threw raki on the dog and set it on fire. The dog howled and died in the flames while the boy watched. 'Abdu! Abdu!' he screamed. Then they beat the boy with clubs until he was senseless. They left him for dead."

Pettigrew leaned forward. He could barely hear. His mind filled in the details.

They were laughing and kicking him with their boots. The boy screamed, and they slapped his head. Back and forth. Back and forth. His teeth were broken; his mouth gaped and dripped with blood.

Kudret put a napkin to his face. Flinders rubbed his nose.

"He did not wake up for days. And when he did, he was a different person. His eyes were wild, and his face was contorted. He thrashed around, striking anyone who came near him. Then he went away."

Pettigrew rubbed his eyes.

The smoke was black and greasy. It smelled of burnt hair. The Cossacks created a monster out of smoke and fire.

Flinders shook the dice.

"'Abdu, Abdu'—I will hear that cry forever." The old man put down the pipe's stem. "I never saw him again until the Bulbul rode through the village. I recognized him as the boy, but the change was horrible. His eyes stared, and his mouth was black."

Kudret peered at the board.

The old man folded his hands. "And that is all I know."

Flinders rolled the dice. "Where was the village?" he asked.

"On the border with Syria."

"Where on the border?"

"To the south. We could see the castle in the distance."

Flinders looked at Pettigrew. "That explains it."

Yes, that explains it.

"Anything else?" the old man asked.

"No. Thank you for the story," Pettigrew said. "I know it was painful to tell, and we are grateful."

"*Teshekkur edderim*," Kudret said, smiling. "Thank you, my friend."

The old man smiled back.

They finished their coffee. Kudret paid the bill and folded the backgammon board. "You are very good." He paused. "For an Englishman."

They rose to leave. Pettigrew looked back as they went out the door, but the old man was gone. A waiter was cleaning the table where he sat. The smell of coffee and tobacco followed them as the door closed. The car was waiting. They walked slowly to it. Its doors squeaked and thumped as they opened them. They got in; the seats were hot.

Pettigrew turned to Flinders. "A haunting story."

"Haunting indeed." Flinders looked out at the crowded street. "The universe turns left here." He settled back in the seat. "But we may not see the face of God."

They drove in silence. The streets were noisy.

They returned to the hotel and had dinner. The dining room glittered. Silver tinkled on china. Conversation drifted in waves. Waiters bowed and polished glasses. Pettigrew ate little.

"I am not hungry," he insisted when Flinders urged him to eat.

They drank a brandy and then went to bed. Pettigrew tossed and dreamed of smoke and fire. He woke up once screaming, "Abdu, Abdu!" Hours passed. A clock chimed in the hallway. Footsteps padded back and forth on the hall carpets and clicked on the tiles.

He heard a soft knock on the door. He thought it was Flinders.

Something has happened.

He opened the door. Gertrude stood before him in the dimly lit hallway. She looked at him with an uncertain smile. Her red hair was down; ringlets trailed on her long coat. She had her fingers in the coat pockets. Pettigrew could see the red nail gloss on her thumbs.

"May I come in?" she said.

"Yes, of course," he answered.

She entered and hesitated. "I heard about the bedawi woman. I wasn't sure."

She unbuttoned her blouse, and he returned to the bed. The gas lamp highlighted her red hair as she approached the bed. She lifted the sheet and slipped beside him.

"Come to me."

After a while, she said, "You are warm."

They lay together, arms about each other.

She sat up and lit a cigarette. "There really is another, isn't there? I could sense it. Just my luck."

Pettigrew started to say something, to tell her it didn't matter, but she put her fingers over his lips. "Don't talk. There is no need." She kissed him. "When I first saw you, I knew." The cigarette glowed. "A woman's instinct."

Then she put the cigarette out and got up. "It could have been so good." She faced him, a pale shadow outlined by the dim lamps. "At least you know that I do not dye my hair."

She pulled on her skirt and buttoned her blouse. She slipped on her shoes and opened the room door. "See you in the morning," she told him, but he did not reply.

The door closed behind her. Pettigrew thought he heard a sob as it closed.

Pettigrew lay back on the pillow and listened to the receding footsteps. What kind of man was he to give up such a woman? She had everything: wealth, education, and status. She knew everybody. Important men sought her out. The world would be hers if she so chose it to be. He pulled up the covers.

But her desperation hides beneath her smile. Her green eyes sparkle, but there is a great darkness behind them. She is both a Damascus blade and a candle guttering in the wind.

Her perfume was still on the pillow.

I would be nothing to her but a trophy to be enjoyed and then cast aside.

He turned over and went to sleep.

The morning came all too early. Pettigrew dressed and went down to the lobby. Through the window, he could see that the gray car was waiting; its yellow spokes gleamed in the sun. Someone had meticulously cleaned them, but he knew they would be dusty again after one drive.

Everything gets dusty here.

Pettigrew opened the ornate hotel doors. Flinders was standing next to the car. He smiled. "Come, get in."

Pettigrew looked up and down the street. Shopkeepers were sweeping the street in front of their stores. Their brooms made scratching noises. Some were setting out baskets of tulips.

What is this place? he thought. He got into the car. The air smelled of leather and seawater, and the wind ruffled his hair. The car started with a shriek of metal and a puff of smoke. They bounced along in silence.

Then Flinders said, "I thought I heard a woman crying in the hall last night. Did you hear anything?"

"No, nothing."

Once again, they returned to the embassy; they were ushered into the room upstairs. Kudret and Gertrude sat waiting. The green eyes stared at Pettigrew; they were expressionless. A marble smile traced her lips.

She does not acknowledge what happened between us last night. Perhaps I do not either.

Pettigrew looked back and then sat down.

"Good morning." Gertrude's voice was a purr.

"Good morning."

"Did you sleep well?"

"Yes. And you?"

"Yes."

Kudret ruffled some papers. "We had some luck," he said. Kudret spread the papers on the table. "A general who hates the Veiled One is willing to talk to us. One of my young men found him. The general likes young men." He smiled. "We obliged him."

Pettigrew looked at Flinders.

"Remember, 'a lake forms drop by drop,'" he added. "He will meet us in an abandoned barracks. We will take a car to the camp." He stood up and ushered them out. "Come."

The green eyes followed Pettigrew.

Flinders looked at Pettigrew. "As Gertrude said, things are done differently here."

Yes, very differently.

"Let us go."

Gertrude followed them downstairs and watched them leave. She did not smile.

Pettigrew turned and watched her still figure through the car's window. The figure grew smaller and smaller.

The car stopped in front of a low-set building, one of several that lined a vacant parade ground. Pettigrew pulled his coat tighter. The grass was long and scarred by patches of raw dirt. Rusted canons stood guard. The setting sun slanted across the building's roof. A fitful breeze fluttered the brims of their hats as they walked.

"These barracks used to house Janissaries, but they are long gone," Kudret told them. "They are used for storage now."

They got out. Somewhere a dog howled. The howl echoed across the parade ground, a lonely sound.

Kudret led them through a door and down a long hall. On one side were closed doors, and on the other were windows grimy with dust. Nothing moved. They reached a door at the end of the hall, and Kudret opened it. The room was small. Pettigrew smelled stale cigarettes and rotting wood. A wooden table and four chairs rested on a bare floor, and a couch stood against a gray wall. The paint had peeled; patches of plaster dotted the walls. The chairs were on one side; the couch was on the other. Its cushions were worn. The bare globe of a gas lamp hung overhead. It was streaked with soot. A dirty window was framed by limp curtains; faint moonlight etched its dull panes. As they entered, the floor creaked.

"This room hasn't been used in years," Kudret said.

They sat in the chairs and waited.

Kudret lit a cigarette. "The general will be here shortly. He speaks English."

Time passed. Kudret smoked another cigarette.

The door opened, and a man in a general's uniform walked in. His hand rested on a holstered pistol.

"This is General Arslan," Kudret said.

The general nodded and sat down on the couch. He placed his fur hat on the table and unbuttoned his blue collar. His gold shoulder braids glistened as he moved. Pettigrew studied his face. A white scar zigzagged down one side of it. He pulled a cigarette from a gold case and carefully lit it; he took a breath and exhaled acrid smoke.

"No one must know that I am here."

"Of course."

He smells of strong cologne, thought Pettigrew.

The general smoothed his pencil mustache with a forefinger and began.

"When I was younger, I commanded a brigade. We were stationed in Iraq, but we were often sent to the Caucasus. We fought many battles against the Russians. Under my command was a young officer, a lieutenant. He was very brave. I decorated him many times. There was also a corporal, a giant of a man. A man who killed for pleasure. The troops were afraid of him, and the sergeants could not discipline him." The general flicked an ash. "He was loyal only to the lieutenant. How they met, I do not know. I think they must have been stationed together somewhere else."

"Please go on."

He took another puff. The cigarette's tip glowed red. "One day, the sultan's personal bodyguard came to the barracks and arrested the officer. The corporal raged and followed them."

A tic pulsed under the general's left eye.

"So the corporal knew the officer from before?"

"I would imagine so."

"Curious. Then what happened?"

"The lieutenant was sentenced to be burned alive, but the corporal helped him to escape. They fled to the south. The lieutenant vowed to kill the sultan and all his family. He convinced opponents of the sultan to join him. Someday, I think he will overthrow the sultan and rule the empire. He rampages the country, and no one dares to oppose him. His agents are everywhere."

Kudret spoke. "We are aware of his activities."

The general straightened his cuffs. The braid, Pettigrew noted, was frayed. "Even the sultan is in fear." The veins in his neck throbbed as he spoke.

"Indeed."

Pettigrew squinted. *Bell taught us that changes in blood pressure indicate the person is lying. I have seen that many times. The general is either lying or omitting something.*

"Yes, you must have seen the patrols. The streets are constantly watched—soldiers are stationed everywhere."

He is preoccupied with patrols. Why?

"We have seen them." Pettigrew fingered his jaw.

"Everyone is in fear." The general pulled out a handkerchief and coughed into it.

He does not look us in the eye, thought Pettigrew. *Not once.*

"Can you tell us where the Veiled One is?" Pettigrew asked.

"He has a villa in the city. It is one of several; he moves between them."

"Will he be there?"

"I do not know," the general replied. "He moves around like a jinn."

"I have heard that before," Pettigrew said.

Another cough. The general put the handkerchief in his pocket.

"Do you have an address?" Flinders asked.

"Yes."

The general slid a small paper across the table and folded his hands as if to protect himself. "Look for this address. It is his villa."

"Is the Veiled One there right now?"

"I do not think so." The general coughed again. "I think he is in the mountains."

Curious.

"Are you sure?"

"Yes."

Even more curious. Why so sure?

"Does the sultan know about this?"

"No."

"Why not?"

Curious that a general in the Turkish army would not inform the sultan.

"There are wheels within wheels, effendi."

I knew it. He leaves something out.

"Wheels within wheels?" Flinders looked at Kudret.

Kudret frowned. "I cannot speak to that."

So, whatever it is, Kudret knows about it as well.

Flinders looked at Pettigrew.

He thinks the same as I do. The general is involved in something, and Kudret knows what it is.

The general leaned forward, his dark eyes pools of worry. "All walls have his ears." He stood and picked up his hat. "I must go now."

The door closed behind him. Only his cigarette smoke remained.

"Do you believe him as to the address?"

"Your eyes are as good as mine," Kudret said with a grin. "And as far as truthfulness is concerned, remember, 'a camel might go to Mecca forty times, but that does not make him a pilgrim.'"

"He gave you a paper."

"All well and good. Now we have a location."

Kudret read the address and then looked up, his eyes wide. "This is next to the sultan's palace." He read the address again. "I think that you Englishmen have a saying . . . something about hiding in plain sight."

Pettigrew smiled. "There may be more about this than a villa hiding in plain sight. It was an American who wrote about a letter that was placed on a table."

"The principle is the same," Flinders mused.

"I will make inquiry." Kudret rose and opened the door. The chairs squeaked as he stood, and the gas lamp flickered.

They followed Kudret out and got in the car. A chill wind whispered across the parade ground. Tips of the ragged grass fluttered and crackled. Faint bugle calls sounded in Pettigrew's imagination.

Kudret spoke. "The Janissaries were once mighty. They marched in silence to a muffled drumbeat. Lines and lines of men who moved in silence."

Pettigrew closed his eyes and saw the shadows moving in unison.

"They almost conquered Europe," Kudret said, turning his head to look out the car window. "Now they are gone. Defeated at last, and by their own people." He slumped in his seat.

He feels the emptiness of history.

The car passed rows of blank windows.

There is a sense of loss here.

Pettigrew thought he saw lights behind them, moving shadows that passed back and forth. But those could have been reflections from the headlights. Or were they?

The drive back to the hotel was long. The streets were dark and cold, the fog from the Bosphorus creeping between the silent buildings and porches. As they entered the hotel, Flinders said, "Someone is planning a coup."

"You feel it too," Pettigrew said and nodded. "We must act before that happens."

Flinders laughed. "Are you sure we're in the right empire?"

"How so?"

Flinders nodded to the doorman.

"The Byzantine Empire," he said. "This feels like Byzantine politics."

"The Byzantine Empire, indeed."

The call to prayer woke Pettigrew. He went to the window and opened it. Sounds of the city flooded the room.

"Get up, get up," the muezzins called. "Prayer is better than sleep. Prayer is better than sleep."

The call carried across the city as minaret after minaret came alive with piety.

Pettigrew knew the words—he had heard them in Cairo years ago. The call echoed and reechoed in his ears. Then it faded and was replaced by the rumble of wheels and cries of street venders. The smell of cooking meat drifted up between the awnings below him. The city was awakening.

He got dressed and went downstairs. The car was waiting. Flinders was already seated. Again, the drive was short. They got out and were directed to a large room on the first floor. Pettigrew peered at a high ceiling covered in frescos and walls lined with baroque chairs with golden arms. A medallioned carpet covered the oak floor. A long table stood on the carpet; rattan chairs surrounded it. Gertrude and Kudret waited at a long buffet. Its top was covered by plates of food and silver pots of coffee and tea.

Pettigrew walked over to the buffet.

The smell of coffee is good in the morning.

"Do have some breakfast," Gertrude said, handing Pettigrew a plate. Her hand shook ever so slightly. "The eggs are excellent. The porridge is over there." She pointed. "Over there are traditional Turkish dishes."

Pettigrew looked. "I see a plate of hummus."

"Yes." She smiled. "I love hummus. I have it every morning." She spooned some onto a plate and handed it to him.

The taste was familiar.

"What is that white paste?" he had asked.

"It is hummus, an Egyptian dish." She had smiled; their heads bent close. "Hummus is Egypt, as I am Egypt."

He took a bite and said, "Then I shall love hummus."

"Do you like it?"

"Yes."

She filled another plate. "Have some bangers."

Their eyes met, and their hands touched under the plate.

"Thank you."

"You are welcome." She managed a tight smile. Pettigrew smiled back.

"More coffee?" she asked.

"Yes, please."

She handed him a cup, and he took it. The cup rattled on its saucer.

"Oh dear," she said, "I have spilled your coffee."

"No, it was my fault."

Kudret waved them to sit. "We have contacted our agent. She speaks English; you can interview her. Come, I will introduce you." He opened the door.

"Mariam, please come in."

A small woman in a white dress with a blue vest and cap entered. She smiled at Flinders. Flinders smiled back.

"Günaydın." Mariam giggled and then curtsied. "Oh, I forgot, you do not speak Turkish. Good morning."

Flinders bowed. "Would you care for some breakfast?"

"Yes, thank you."

"I will get a plate."

She brushed a stray curl of black hair under her cap. The coins on it jingled. She sat down, and Flinders sat next to her. He set the plate before her.

"You do not wear a veil?"

"I do when I am in the street. I am an Assyrian."

"Assyrian? I though they vanished centuries ago."

"You are looking at one now, effendi." She fluttered her gray eyes. "Do you like what you see?"

"I do. Coffee?"

"Yes, please."

"Do go on."

"My name is Mariam. My parents brought me here from Urmia when I was a little girl. Assyrians have lived in Urmia from time immemorial."

"I know something of Assyrians." Flinders lifted his cup. "I helped curate the Assyrian collection at the museum." He raised his cup. "They were an impressive civilization many centuries ago." Then he smiled. "But you are here."

"I came years ago." She picked up a napkin and smoothed it over her lap.

"And you learned to belly dance?"

She nodded, and her long ringlets swayed. "Among other things."

"Some eggs?" Flinders asked.

"Thank you."

Flinders turned from the buffet and handed her a plate. The plate slipped; she caught it and laughed.

"Oh, I am sorry."

"Your hand is cold."

"It is a cold morning."

"You were saying?"

"I teach the harem girls to dance. The girls come in from the country. Their fathers are shaykhs or pashas. The girls are the payments that cement alliances. They are pretty, but they have no skills—they cannot attract the eye of the master." She laughed. "Harems are places of intrigue and power. A seductive woman can become mother to a prince, or even a sultan. The stakes are very high, and the women are very aggressive. They use their sex as a weapon."

"Indeed."

She arched an eyebrow. "Do your English women have such skills, effendi?"

Touché.

"Biscuit?"

"Please."

She laughed. "Without skills, they will always be ladies in waiting, mere maids to the women in power." Her eyes twinkled. "The harem is a ruthless place, effendi."

"Ruthless?"

She patted Flinders's arm. Flinders did not move.

"People mysteriously disappear, effendi."

"Disappear?"

She took his hand. "Only the Bosphorus knows how many sacks have been thrown in it. Sometimes the sacks float, and sometimes they sink."

"But there are guards."

"The eunuchs, effendi."

Flinders put his fork down. "Eunuchs?"

Ms. Barra has a rival. Flinders seems unusually naive.

"Men who have been altered in different ways," Mariam said and giggled again.

"Altered in different ways?"

Her eyes twinkled. "Yes, according to their duties."

"I see, so that they will not make advances on the women?"

She sipped her coffee. "You have it backward, effendi." She laughed. "So that the women will not be able to seduce them."

Flinders, you have met your match.

"Ham?" Flinders said, offering her a piece—then quickly, "Oh, I am sorry."

"I eat ham." She smiled. "I am a Christian. My people were converted at the time of Christ."

Flinders handed her the plate. "Oh, excuse me."

"It is all right. My hand is now warm." She leaned close. "Now, what do you want to know, effendi?"

"Can you get into the Veiled One's harem?"

"Of course, effendi. I have been there many times."

"There is a statue of a woman with a snake curled around her."

"I think I have seen it."

"Can you show us where it is?"

"Of course, effendi."

"Have you seen the Veiled One?"

Her eyes darkened. "No. But I heard his clogs once before the eunuchs made me leave."

"Clogs?"

"Yes, effendi. He wears clogs to announce his entrance to the harem. The sultan wears them also. The noise of the clogs alerts the women to his presence so that they can prepare themselves."

Clogs, is it? Flinders, you are lost.

Her eyes danced. "Would you like to wear clogs, effendi?"

Flinders started to say something and then stopped.

Flinders, whatever happened to your wit and charm?

"The harem is a wonderous place." Mariam's eyes were roguish. "And if I take you there, what will be my reward, effendi?"

"We will take care of that," Kudret interrupted. "We will contact you when we are ready to enter the harem."

Flinders stood up and shook her hand.

They hold hands a little too long.

She smiled and left—a flash of silk and a breath of perfume.

Flinders stared after her. The door closed.

Gertrude followed his eyes. "She is beautiful, isn't she?"

Kudret laughed. "Be careful, effendi. Assyrians are famous warriors, and so are their women. You might find her more difficult than you think."

Coffee flowed. Waiters refilled the buffet. Silver lids clinked. The smell of sausages and eggs filled the room. Traffic noise hummed through the tall windows. Sunlight moved across the rose medallions in the rug. The conversation turned to the Veiled One's harem.

"A harem? Now, how are we supposed to get in there, even with Mariam's help?" Pettigrew asked. "We cannot just walk in, you know."

"That will not be difficult." Kudret smiled. "You have been reading too many adventure stories." He drank some coffee. "Harems are not all about unclothed ladies dancing in front of turbaned men. They are humdrum places where there is nothing to do."

He put the cup down. "The ladies of the harem are bored. They want entertainment. Troops of dancers are always welcome; my dancers are often invited."

"But what about us?"

"You will go disguised as koceks." Kudret grinned. "I have some costumes that might fit you."

"Disguised as belly dancers?" Flinders asked, his eyes bright.

Pettigrew snorted. "I do not think so." Then he chuckled. "Besides, we look a little old for the part."

"Nonsense, you will make a fine-looking dancer," Flinders said. "I can hardly contain myself." He laughed. "You will be a boy with curls again."

"With wrinkles and stubble."

"Some earrings, some ringlets, and a touch of makeup." Flinders grinned at the thought. "You will look like a choirboy."

"I thought I looked like Thutmose."

"You will be a young and blond Thutmose."

An aging Thutmose.

"Yes, the guards will think that you are a Circassian," Kudret said. He laughed. "Blond dancers are very sought after," he added. "As you English would say, 'They are all the rage.'"

Flinders grinned. "We can wear makeup, like actors."

"First robes, now this."

"You liked the robes, and the dance costume is only to get us past the guards."

Pettigrew frowned. "I'm not an actor," he grumbled.

"We will go tonight," Flinders stated.

And so it was.

NINE

A Sacred and Forbidden Place

They gathered at the embassy. Mariam wore a cloak with a white veil and a red skirt over harem pants. Flinders and Pettigrew were dressed as koceks. Both wore red.

Flinders twisted his large gold earrings. "Just like a pirate." He spread out the baggy pants. "Look at the knee room. I wonder what my tailor could do with these."

"You want a kocek's costume tailored?" Gertrude shook her head.

"This might set a new fashion in London."

"How so?" Pettigrew chimed in.

"Men's pants are too tight; making the pants fuller would liberate them."

"I have heard of your Beau Brummell," Kudret said with a laugh, "but I did not think that I would meet him."

"Indeed, you may have." Gertrude giggled. "Imagine sneaking into a heavily guarded harem with Beau Brummell at your side." Her green eyes flashed. "I would love to go along." She winked at Flinders. "Especially with such a well-tailored man." She frowned. "But the ambassador has forbidden it."

Kudret's eyes twinkled. "I see that the staff has groomed you," he said. "Your hair should be a little longer, but that will have to do."

"Thomas, let me look at you," Flinders said, grinning from ear to ear.

The war horse chomps at the bit.

"Indeed, you do look lovely this evening." He peered at Pettigrew with amusement. "That red cap with the coins suits you marvelously. Those trousers are wonderful. And that skirt sets them off beautifully."

Pettigrew growled. "I have enough makeup on to sink HMS *Victory*."

Flinders played with his castanets in response.

Mariam laughed. "Follow me." She curved her arms and clashed her finger cymbals.

"That's better." Her eyes twinkled. "You are a natural kocek, effendi."

She took off her cloak and veil and began to move rapidly around the room with short, bouncing steps. Her high heels syncopated on the floor. Her earrings flashed, and her dark curls swung from side to side. "Now, follow my hips."

Flinders copied her.

"No, no, lift your hips—don't drop them." She spun into a backbend. "Move, effendi."

Pettigrew watched.

Flinders, sometimes you surprise me.

"Yes, he was quite the dancer at Oxford," Pettigrew said.

I cannot not resist.

"The ladies loved to dance with him." He laughed. "Perhaps the ladies of the harem will want to dance with him also."

Kudret smiled. "Perhaps so, effendi. Perhaps so."

His eyes clouded over. "But to be a true kocek, some sacrifices are required."

The boy said the shears were cold.

Flinders closed his castanets.

Mariam's eyes flashed. "Now, effendi, we will have some excitement."

Flinders grinned.

He has found a kindred spirit.

Kudret was impatient. "Enough, we need to go."

Pettigrew wrapped a saber in a roll of capes. "A little old-fashioned but effective." He smiled. "And quiet." He looked at Flinders. "If we use pistols, their thunder will bring the walls down and the guards running."

The flashes bounced off the walls; peels of thunder shook the floor. Pale faces with staring eyes flickered in and out of the darkness.

"We can't have a repeat of what happened in the catacombs of Alexandria."

"These machine pistols are quieter." Flinders examined the pistol Woolley had given him. "I shall bring them anyway."

Gertrude held the door open and ushered them through. Her eyes never left Pettigrew. As he passed her, he thought he heard her whisper, "Be careful. You are my opal." But it might have been the wind.

The streets were cold and empty as the car rolled along. Flashes of lightning outlined the domes and minarets. Fog swirled in sheets in front of them. They sat close, not breathing. The dark buildings flowed past.

"I have an uneasy feeling about this," Pettigrew whispered to Flinders.

"I know, but we must go on."

The car let them out at the end of a narrow, cobblestoned alley. Cobbles glistened in the moonlight, shining silver and black shapes before Pettigrew's eyes.

I saw cobbles like these once before.

The street was a canyon between buildings that twisted and turned as they walked. A ribbon of pale light streamed above jagged rooftops. Their steps echoed hollowly.

"This is the Street of the Eunuchs," Kudret said, pointing. "From here they can enter harems unseen. They have been walking this street for hundreds of years. The very cobbles are worn from their footsteps. If these cobbles could talk, what would they say?" He smiled. "Now you will add to these footsteps."

He went on. "We will not be noticed. Any guards that see us will think we are coming to dance."

They walked under overhanging porches and passed by rows of silent doors. Faint music and laughter crept out into the street. A solitary cat strolled across their way, its tail curled in the dim light.

Kudret stopped at an iron-studded door.

"Be quiet and let us do the talking." He knocked.

Flinders chuckled. "And, Thomas, please do try to look charming."

The heavy door opened. Light streamed out and splashed on the cobbles behind them. A face under a tall hat peered at them.

Mariam spoke to it and then turned to face them when the man ushered them inside and left them near the entrance.

"I told him that the master had requested a private performance for the delight of his wives."

Blue-coated guards lounged about; their fezzes lay on the floor next to them. Other guards sat at a low table and played backgammon. They laughed and slammed the pieces. A few dozed in chairs, their legs spread out before them, their scimitars resting on their stomachs. Cigarette smoke curled lazily; the room smelled of raki.

Kudret touched a guard on the arm and winked. He wiggled his hips. The guard smiled, said a word, and stood back.

Mariam spoke again and then translated. "He says that the harem is up those stairs." She pointed to a two-story archway tiled in blue and white.

Two guards in white uniforms stood before the door. They frowned and crossed their scimitars. One of them said something. Mariam spoke softly to him and giggled.

"He wants to know why the blond dancer is so tall. I told them you were a Circassian from a very tall family. And that you float like foam on the sea when you dance."

Flinders smiled. "She has that right—like foam on the sea."

Pettigrew said nothing.

The guards grinned and put up their scimitars.

"Come, we must hurry," Kudret cautioned. "The Bulbul is somewhere in this villa."

They ran up the stairs and knocked on a bronze door. A slit opened, and a girl's face looked out. Her eyes were suspicious.

Mariam smiled and said something. A bolt was withdrawn with a clang, and the door slowly opened.

"I told her that we had come to entertain the wives," Mariam explained.

"She is the daughter of one of them." A waft of perfume and incense blew over them. The air was warm.

Flinders sniffed and asked Mariam, "What is this lovely smell?"

"You are entering the world of women, effendi."

They entered.

A girl of fifteen, dressed in blue, stood in front of them. She skipped and laughed and led them down a wide hall.

She is young and happy, Pettigrew mused. *I was young once.*

A hallway opened before them. Wooden pillars supported beamed arches above them. Vases of tulips and other flowers stood guard. Faint music and singing drifted through the archways. Wooden balconies with carved railings, also of wood, lined the sides of the hall. Silk-clad women, a rainbow of reds and greens and blues, walked about in front of them and then stopped and looked.

"They see a troupe of dancers," Kudret said.

Other women came out of doors and leaned over the railings. They clapped and cheered; their bracelets jingled. Children ran out from under the balconies. They screamed and laughed.

"The koceks are here! The koceks are here!"

Flinders seemed surprised. "They seem very enthusiastic."

"Their lives are empty and lonely," Mariam said.

"I thought they lived in great luxury and ease."

"That is Western nonsense. They live in small apartments with their children." Mariam sighed. "Every day is the same for them."

Flinders looked surprised. "But I have seen paintings—acres of tiles, nude women bathing, and men in large turbans leering."

"Imagination, effendi."

Flinders insisted. "There was a snake charmer, a naked boy with a serpent wrapped around him. Men stared at him."

"More imagination."

"But I read about harems in *The Arabian Nights*."

"You mean *The Book of the Thousand Nights and One Night*?" She laughed. "Those are fables—Scheherazade did not exist."

"Are you so sure?"

Pettigrew scowled. "Never mind Scheherazade. Remember why we are here."

Mariam grinned, ignoring Pettigrew. "Folktales from the Abbasid Empire . . . stories of love and lust, effendi."

"They seemed so real."

"Aladdin was a myth, effendi." She grasped his hand and squeezed it. "No Westerner has ever been permitted inside a harem. You and your friend may be the first."

Flinders nodded and made as though to walk ahead.

"Follow me," Mariam told him.

They passed an archway. Its sides were covered in blue-and-white tile. A woman with wet hair and a towel lounged against the tile. She wore red slippers and nothing else. Behind her, Pettigrew could hear laughing and splashing. Flinders stared at her.

Mariam followed his eyes. "She shaves so that she will be smooth to the touch." She arched an eyebrow. "Do not your Englishwomen do the same for you?" She pouted. "No?"

"At least I have not seen it myself."

"Poor effendi."

"This is a small harem. There are less than fifty women here," she added. "They are the daughters of the Veiled One's allies. The sultan's harem has more than three thousand women. There women are educated and can marry young officials and enter the bureaucracy themselves. Here there is only tedium and unsatisfied urges."

"Tedium?"

"Yes, effendi," Mariam said with a sigh. "You cannot imagine the loneliness and the longing."

"They are all young. I do not see any older women."

"There are older wives, but you will not see them," Mariam said. "They are lost."

"Lost?"

"Yes, their beauty has left them, so they can no longer charm. Their children have gone. They live alone in their apartments."

"How terrible."

"Old age is terrible."

Indeed so.

"Is there nothing for them?"

"The harem is a cruel place, effendi."

A tall woman with a high green hat and long dress approached them. She spoke briefly with Kudret and then pointed. Her jewels twinkled with reds and greens.

Flinders looked at Mariam.

"She is the valide, the mother," Mariam explained. "She rules the harem. Harems are well organized. Everyone here has her place."

"It is like an army."

"Yes, effendi, an army of women."

"Where do they march?"

"They march nowhere, effendi."

"Come on, enough of this talk. This way." Kudret pushed them along.

At the end of the hall was a double door covered with gold carvings.

"This leads to the covered courtyard where the dancers perform."

They hurried toward it. Women came down wooden stairs and followed them, chattering and laughing. Some carried babies; others led their children by the hand. Beaded caps bobbed, skirts and vests rippled, and bracelets dangled—a moving sea of silk, jewels flashing on its waves. Perfume filled the hall.

A small girl in a blue dress took Pettigrew's hand. She looked up at him and smiled. He looked down and smiled back.

"They follow us."

"Yes, effendi, they follow us."

Mariam shook her head playfully. "Are you surprised?"

As they reached the doors, Kudret stopped and put his hands on his head.

"Where is the orchestra?" He looked up at the balconies. "Ladies, we will have to wait for the orchestra to arrive." He waved at the crowd of women and children. "Wait for us here. We will loosen our joints in the hall." He opened the door. He strutted and danced; he smiled and blew kisses. "Be patient with us. Quickly now." He slid a bar and held the door open. "We do not have much time."

They entered. Space opened in front of them. Red and gold ridges marched across a two-story barreled ceiling. Brown-and-green tiles checkered the floor. A procession of columns with locus caps receded in the distance. Tall arches covered in tile and gold lettering in Arabic script dotted the walls. A large marble fountain splashed. Benches in gold and brown circled the walls. Pettigrew smelled incense and flowers.

Opulent, indeed.

High up from the floor, a balcony ran along one side of the vast room. Wooden screens hid a series of tall openings.

Mariam followed Pettigrew's eyes. "The Veiled One sits concealed behind the screens and picks out a woman for the night," she explained.

They continued across the hall. Behind them, another door opened, and women streamed in. Children spread out across the room, chasing each other and laughing.

"They come." Mariam smiled. "They are expecting a grand performance, effendi." She looked at Flinders. The gray eyes twinkled over the veil. "Are you up for such a performance, effendi?"

Flinders looked around.

"Can you give these women something to remember?" Mariam wiggled her hips. "Perhaps something like this?"

She danced a few steps, and three teenage girls in blue imitated her movements. Flinders took the hands of two seven-year-old girls in blue and swept them with him.

Pettigrew felt a tug and looked down. The girl in blue had been replaced by a very serious face—a young boy wearing a gray gallabiyah trotted beside him. The face stared enviously at Pettigrew's necklace. Pettigrew took off his necklace and placed it around the boy's neck. The boy fingered it and laughed. Another boy tried to grab it. The first boy pushed him away, and he fell down.

Pettigrew held out his hand. The boy seized it; the serious face smiled.

They danced forward, and the women and children danced with them.

We are leading a children's crusade. What kind of man am I to lead children like this?

Tiles stretched before them. At the far end, they saw a small alcove. Two leafy palm trees in golden bowls framed its entrance. Pots of fresh flowers lined the opening.

Mariam pointed. "Look! Is that what you want?"

They rushed to it and then stopped, stunned by what they saw. A painting of a pleasant woman with smiling eyes, short dark hair, and a wide hat looked back at them. Her smile was calm.

"This is the Veiled One's mother," Kudret whispered.

She looks out from the photograph. Her eyes remind me of my mother. My father came to the cricket field. "Your mother is dead," he said. I remember that moment; I know how the Veiled One must have felt.

Candles burned on either side of her.

Mariam said, "He never lets them go out."

Aphrodite stood on a low law table in front of the portrait. The serpent curled around the white marble. Aphrodite smiled at Pettigrew. The snake eyes were wide.

It is just like the dream.

The laughing stopped.

Mariam turned and covered her eyes as tears flowed down her cheeks.

Kudret muttered, "There is no wise proverb to explain what I see."

Flinders frowned. "Even monsters have hearts."

Pettigrew stared. "I would not have expected this." He looked up. "From where he sat in the balcony, he could always see her." He shook his head.

What kind of man sits and watches this? Kudret said that he watched his mother die in agony. Now he watches her smile at him forever. That could be me.

The women and children crowded behind them. They murmured among themselves.

Flinders recovered. "We cannot wait."

He stepped forward and pushed the pots aside. He seized the statue.

"We must act."

The crowd shrank back. A woman screamed. More women added their voices; a chorus of screams echoed off the walls.

"Quickly now," Kudret urged. "The noise will bring the guards."

"Too late!" Pettigrew saw that a door had burst open, and several guards in red charged through it.

The guards yelled and ran forward. Their scimitars flashed. The women scattered.

Flinders handed the statue to Kudret. "Hold this."

Flinders frowned at the onrushing guards. "They need a good tailor. Their pants are entirely too large." He reached for his pistol.

Pettigrew blocked his hand. "Wait. If you use that, you will wake the entire villa." He pulled the saber from the clothes. "Let me use this."

Flinders snatched it. "My turn."

He smoothed his hair back under the cap, flourished the saber, and then charged the guards. His skirt billowed. Women scrambled out of his way.

"Dost thou complain about my nose?" He slashed the nearest guard. The guard screamed and fell.

"You say, 'No wind, O majestic nose'?" Flinders parried a blow and thrust home. Swords clanged. His gold vest glinted. A second guard fell.

He pivoted, the jewels on his cap flashing. "When it bleeds, such a Red Sea!" he cried. The third guard clutched his stomach, groaned, and staggered back. Flinders paused for breath and then effortlessly slapped a scimitar aside.

Women shrieked.

"'Point it against the cavalry,' you say?" Flinders slashed again. A fourth slumped. Flinders whirled the saber and bounded forward. His feet tattooed the tiles, now slippery with blood.

The remaining guards fled. Their scimitars rattled on the floor.

He saluted with the saber. "And now my nose is at peace."

Screams bounced off the walls. Children cried. Women ran from the hall. Silks flashed. Arms and legs blurred. Scarfs, shoes, and jewelry littered the cold marble.

Flinders lowered the saber and straightened his sleeves. He put a hand to his neck and said, "I think my necklace is broken."

"We must leave at once," Kudret said, beckoning them toward the entrance.

"Well, that was certainly spectacular." Pettigrew laughed. "And done in costume, too."

Flinders took a couple of heavy breaths. "I have my moments," he said.

"Like the old days."

Pettigrew pushed Mariam and Kudret toward the ornate door.

"But the poetry?" Mariam asked.

Flinders leaned against the edge of the fountain. "A seventeenth-century French poet and swordsman with a big nose."

"A poet?"

"With a big nose."

Flinders fled the scene, and Pettigrew followed.

"Flinders, I was worried about you years ago when you planned to become a necromancer. But now you attack harem guards and spout poetry about a nose."

Pettigrew slammed the ornate door behind them and slid its bar into place to lock it. "This should stay the guards for a bit. But about the nose," Pettigrew said, pushing them forward. "Where did you get that from?"

They ran under the balconies. They passed the doorway with the fountains. Water arced and glittered. Shrieks replaced laughter; a towel lay abandoned on the tile. Women ran under the balconies and darted into their rooms. Some pushed their children ahead of them. Other children lost in the rush tumbled out of their way. A toddler dragging a fallen scimitar ran behind them on short legs. The blade scraped on the tile. It tangled his legs, and he fell.

Mariam stopped, turned, and ran back. Flinders waited. She rescued him from the blade's razor edge and hurried back to Flinders.

"A mother's instinct," she said unapologetically.

"The nose, the nose," Flinders said, putting a finger alongside his nose. "A nose for all seasons." He grinned. "Now, if you don't mind"—Flinders pulled at an ear—"these earrings are extremely uncomfortable."

Pettigrew avoided a baby on the floor.

"And where did you learn to fence like that?"

He picked up the baby and handed the child to the distraught mother. She screamed and fled.

Flinders held Mariam's hand. The two young girls were still holding the other one—she smiled and pushed them gently away.

Flinders laughed. "How quickly they forget."

"Forget?"

Flinders dusted himself off. "What did you once say? That the French believe that you should dispatch an opponent without wrinkling your cuffs?" Flinders twirled the saber. "Remember, I was captain of the Oxford fencing team. 'The best fencer in decades,' the coach said. The saber was my specialty. We trained to these verses."

A small boy blocked his way. Flinders dropped the saber, scooped him up on the run, and kissed him on his cheeks. "You are very bold, my friend. But not tonight." He put the boy down. The boy ran off.

"Ah, yes." Pettigrew laughed. "Now I remember. You used to practice lunging at the walls of our rooms. Plaster would fly about. Other students would complain about the noise."

"Hurry, effendis," Mariam urged them.

"She is right," Pettigrew said. "You do talk too much."

The bronze door blocked them.

"What about the women? They will alert the guards."

"Do not worry—they will not call out," Kudret reassured them. "They have been confined for too long. They will hide in their apartments."

"Curious. They are like birds who stay in the cage, even though its door is open."

"They have nowhere else to go, effendi." Mariam looked at the floor. "They have been here too long. There is nothing for them outside the harem."

She turned back for a moment. "The harem is its own world, effendi."

They pushed the heavy bronze door. It swung open slowly. They looked down the stairs. The guards looked back. Backgammon dice clicked. Scimitars had fallen off the sleeper's stomachs. "Best to let sleeping guards lie," Flinders said, grinning.

"Well, poet or not, nose or not, we must go." Pettigrew pushed them through the doors. "The Bulbul will be here any second now. And I do not think that either your poet or his nose can stop him."

"Now comes the tricky part," Kudret said. "Compose yourselves." He smoothed his jacket. "Try to look nonchalant."

The bronze door slammed shut behind them. Two of the guards opened their eyes.

"They are waking up," Flinders looked at Kudret.

"Smile and be happy."

They crept down the stairs.

"Wait." Kudret blocked them with his hand. "I will distract them." He bounced down the stairs. He wiggled his hips. He lunged and spread his legs. His castanets crackled, and his arms were waves of motion. He pouted and blew kisses.

The guards grinned at him. The backgammon players stopped and looked. They shook their dice cups and called out. Some sleepers picked up their scimitars. One of the guards reached out. Kudret shifted a hip. The guard missed his grip, staggered, and fell. Other guards raised their raki glasses and cheered. They cleared a path. Kudret turned and waved the troupe to come.

"Impressive, if I must say," Pettigrew whispered.

Kudret smiled. "I am a little rusty."

"Nonsense."

"Now that I am a director, I sit at a desk all day."

Flinders laughed. "I sit at a desk all day, too. But not today. Maybe never again."

They descended the stairs and slithered by the guards. Mariam smiled. Kudret waved daintily, and Flinders nodded politely. Pettigrew managed a "pleasant" expression—though it was hard for him to gauge, without a mirror, how pleasant it truly was.

They closed the iron-studded door and began to run. The street breathed relief. Their footsteps clattered on the cobbles. Moonlight threw distorted shadows in front of them. The street was endless; they became breathless. They were halfway down the alley when the iron door clanged open. Light flooded the street. The clang echoed in their ears, and they turned to look.

A roar carried down the street. Waves of anger swept the cobbles. Buildings shivered.

The Bulbul's giant figure was silhouetted against the light. With one hand, he dragged a girl by the hair. They froze at the sight.

"That is the girl who let us in," said Flinders.

Pettigrew felt a lump form in his throat.

She screamed and struggled. The Bulbul smiled, and then he picked the girl up with a hand around her neck. Her feet kicked. He grabbed the top of her head and wrenched it. Her legs jerked, and she went limp. He threw her body at them. It hit the cobbles with a lifeless thud, arms and legs at odd angles—a rag doll in a blue dress. Jewelry scattered and rolled across the street.

You monster. It was all Pettigrew could think.

Mariam screamed and covered her eyes. Kudret turned away.

The Bulbul spat and pointed a finger at Pettigrew.

"He remembers you from the castle." Flinders's jaw clenched. "I do not think that he likes you."

Pettigrew stared. "We will meet again. Next time will be different."

Very different. I'll be ready for you this time.

"Run!" cried Kudret, and they did.

Pettigrew ran, his heart pounding.

She screamed; my heart exploded in my chest. I held her. My heart thumped with pain. I could not help; my world grew dark as I watched her agony.

They ran down the crooked street and reached the gray car, their doors slamming almost simultaneously in their scramble to escape. Yellow spokes spun, and the car lurched into gear.

Pettigrew looked back. The narrow mouth of the alley had receded, and the Bulbul stood panting in a circle of streetlight. He shook his fists and raged at them. Slowly, the furious figure grew smaller. The car turned a corner. Pettigrew faced front. Crooked streets swam before them. Crossing guards in black uniforms shouted and jumped out of the way. After some distance, Kudret shouted, "Stop here!"

Kudret and Mariam climbed out.

"Do not worry about us," Kudret said as he helped Mariam get out. "We will take care of Mariam."

Flinders caught Mariam's hand. "We will meet again."

"God willing," she said. She smiled and kissed him on the cheek.

Pettigrew shook Kudret's hand. "Goodbye, my friend. And please say goodbye to Gertrude for me."

"Yes, goodbye. I will do so." Kudret paused a moment and then said, "But remember, 'a snake is not taken with the hand.' The Bulbul will follow you. You have taken his master's treasure, and he intends to get it back." He let go of Pettigrew's hand. "I will worry."

"You have my word"—Pettigrew ground his teeth—"that he will not succeed."

"Drive on."

The car started. Exhaust billowed. Flinders fingered the rouge on his cheek. Pettigrew looked back. Kudret and Mariam waved through the back window and then disappeared into the darkness. The street was empty.

"A strong man," said Pettigrew.

"Indeed. And generous of spirit."

"And a beautiful woman."

"Yes."

"I think that you will miss her."

Flinders sighed. "I already do."

Pettigrew turned and peered out the windscreen. "Where are we going?"

"Back to Carchemish."

"We don't have enough petrol."

"Nonsense, I stuffed the boot with cans of petrol. Now stop arguing."

The trip was long and hot. The car jostled. Pettigrew sometimes slept. A rag doll in a blue dress haunted his dreams. Jewels sparkled and splashed across a cobbled street. A black mouth swelled and gaped. He woke up with his shirt soaked with sweat. He rubbed his eyes and curled up against the side of the car. Its metal was hard against his face.

TEN

Now Set the Teeth

The desert unrolled before them, harsh, pitiless, and empty. Pettigrew was groggy from lack of sleep. Flies tried to settle on his eyes. Strange buildings loomed before him. The heat was oppressive; reality wavered. Lights flashed before his eyes.

Then Flinders grabbed the windscreen. "I see black tents. They look familiar."

The gray car rolled to a stop. Women and children crowded around it. "Ya, ya, Abul hol."

Flinders grinned. "They seem to know you, Abul hol."

They got out and staggered into a tent. Unayza steadied Pettigrew. They collapsed into sleep.

A day passed. Then another. Nothing moved in the desert heat. Bright sun turned the dunes into waves of sand and shadow.

"Wake up."

Pettigrew's eyes fluttered open. Lawrence was standing over him, shaking him awake. "You must get up. Flinders is already dressed."

Unayza poured water from a long-necked ewer into a bowl. Pettigrew splashed his face and slicked back his hair. The water was icy cold. She held out a sword.

"She wants you to take it," Lawrence said. "It belonged to her grandfather. He fought many battles."

Pettigrew took the sword and strapped it on. It was heavy. Unayza smiled, but her face was wet with tears.

Lawrence loaded two pistols. "The horizon is filled with camels. They will overwhelm us. The shaykh has ordered the women and children to stay in their tents." As he spoke, women ran through the camp, clutching their babies and crying. Children screamed for their lost mothers. Men saddled camels.

Lawrence loaded two more pistols. "The men will form a line. Come on. Bring your pistols. We will make them pay for this."

They mounted and rode to the edge of the camp. Lawrence and Flinders were abreast of Pettigrew. Flinders saluted with his saber. "We will die like men, my friend."

Camels passed them and dust covered them. Rider after rider joined the line. Some hung back and stretched out their hands to women in black. The hands met in one last touch. Harnesses jingled as the riders plodded into line. Small boys and girls ran up to them. Riders leaned down, patted them on the head, and pushed them back to their waiting mothers.

"They say goodbye to their sons and daughters," Lawrence said.

The camels stuttered and groaned. Slanting sun rays cast shadows beneath their splayed feet.

The shaykh pulled his sword. "We go now, my friends." He raised the sword. "*Hafzakem allah*—may God protect you."

The line began to move. Sword blades flashed in the waning light.

"Wait." Lawrence shielded his eyes. "There is a rider out there."

A solitary camel and rider stood at the top of a dune.

Lawrence turned to Pettigrew. "It is the Bulbul. He is alone. He challenges you to single combat. It is an ancient challenge, one worthy only of warriors. You are honored, my friend."

"Am I honored?"

"He waits."

"There is no choice, then. I must go."

"Ya, ya, Abul hol," the people around him cheered.

Pettigrew leaned over and patted Nellie on her neck. "Are you ready to die with me?" Nellie burped. "I will take that as a yes."

You are a good friend, Nellie; I will bring you back. He spurred her forward.

"Ya, ya, Abul hol," Lawrence called after him.

Camels slithered aside, and the line opened a space for him to pass. He rode through it as Nellie plodded rhythmically forward. The horizon swayed from side to side.

"Ya, ya, Abul hol."

They chant; they cheer for me. But I am only a man, and the creature on the hill is a monster. I did not ask for this.

Women in black streamed out from the tents. They surrounded Nellie. They warbled with an undulating trill.

An eerie sound.

More and more women joined in. They crowded around him; some touched the camel. Then they fanned out across the sand. Their voices reached a crescendo as he passed and then spread into the emptiness behind him as he entered the desert. The voices carried him forward. The sound echoed again and again, rising and falling, across the dunes.

The shaykh bowed his head as Pettigrew passed. "They celebrate the great warrior who rides into battle," he told him. "They have done so for a thousand years."

"*Inshallah*; if Allah wills it." The shaykh drew his sword.

"Pray for our salvation." Pettigrew rode through. Nellie plodded rhythmically forward. The horizon swayed from side to side.

"Ya, ya, Abul hol."

I cannot fail you. I failed once before, but I cannot fail again. She died, but these people will not die.

"Ya, ya Abul hol."

I must not fail you.

"Ya, ya, Abul hol."

Pettigrew straightened in the saddle.

I shall not fail you.

The women's voices faded. Pettigrew saw the solitary rider. The Bulbul waited on his camel, a motionless black figure. His upraised sword glowed red in the setting sun. The distance shortened. Waves of dunes flowed past Pettigrew. The sky reddened in front of him. He felt time slow to a crawl. The jingle of the bit rang like a church bell in his ears. The arm that held the sword throbbed, and his skin prickled with a thousand itches. Dry paper filled his mouth.

Am I a man?

The two riders faced each other.

Pettigrew reined in. "You will find my arm heavier this time." He kicked Nellie into a run. Sand splashed fountains of gold.

"Now!"

They closed the difference.

Dust swirled and enveloped the struggling figures. Swords twisted like tongues of flame. They clashed and sparked. Curses rang out. Hammer blows drove Pettigrew back and Nellie to her knees.

"Get up, get up!" he cried, until she righted.

Riders parted, whirled, and charged again and again. The Bulbul ripped Pettigrew's kufiyah off and spit in his face. His black mouth gaped and grinned. Camels ground together, snapping and biting. They groaned and spit. Their legs splayed and sent gouts of sand and rocks flying. The sun sunk lower, the brown dust turning to iron. Writhing shadows stretched and twined against the fading rays; distorted outlines streamed in waves across the ground. The air grew cold.

A terrible tiredness set in.

I cannot do it. But I must do it. She would wish me to succeed.

Pettigrew turned toward Nellie. Her ribs heaved, and she staggered with fatigue. Her breath came in hoarse gulps. "One more time. Just one more time."

They closed in again. The sword arced downward; the Bulbul's camel missed a step and swerved. Pettigrew parried the wide swinging blade and slashed. The Bulbul slumped sideways and fell. The camels passed and drew apart.

"Down, Nellie!" Pettigrew yelled, sliding from her back. He ran to the fallen figure. Dust puffed from his strides. He kicked the Bulbul's sword away and hammered the fallen figure with his fists. Back and forth, from left fist to right, again and again, screaming with each stroke. "You killed that girl for no reason! No reason at all!"

A red circle spread in the sand. Pettigrew picked up his sword and raised it.

The brown eyes opened wide; the broken mouth whispered, "Abdu, Abdu, I come to you."

Pettigrew clutched the handle with both hands and drove the blade into the Bulbul's chest. He dropped to his knees. He rose and half-crawled to Nellie. "We did it!" And he collapsed against the saddle with his arm around her neck.

What have I done? Would she have wanted this?

The sword fell from his hand.

What have I become?

The sun set and the air grew chill. The vault glittered. Somewhere a dog howled in the emptiness. The howl echoed across the dunes. It faded as Pettigrew's vision clouded.

His world turned black.

"Ya, ya, Abul hol."

The noise awakened him.

"Ya, ya, Abul hol."

He opened his eyes. Women and children were crowding around him. He felt a tug. The boy who was not sick held his hands. Pettigrew tousled the boy's hair. "I see that you have recovered." Nellie twisted her head around to look.

Flinders helped him to rise, and Pettigrew put his arms around his shoulder. "We searched all over for you."

The two staggered toward the black tents. The boy who was not sick trudged behind them, leading Nellie. Blood spotted the sand.

"Please take care of Nellie," Pettigrew said, his voice a hoarse whisper. "She has been bitten."

"You have been wounded."

"It's just a scratch."

"Of course it is."

My arm hurts. My back hurts. I hurt everywhere.

The procession slowly wound its way back. The rising sun lit its path. Bands of light layered the sky behind the walkers. Golden shadows danced across the sand and crinkled in front of them. Morning chill gave way to a welcome warmth. The tent was dark and warm. Through half-closed eyes, Pettigrew saw Unayza bending over him. His eyes closed. Her smile was etched on his lids.

He fell into an uneasy sleep. At times, when he startled awake, he could smell Unayza's perfume on his pillow. His dreams were nightmares. The Bulbul towered over him. His mouth gaped black and screamed. Pettigrew twisted and turned. Shadows flashed in his mind. Knights drummed. The old man with the challis floated past his eyes. A girl in blue smiled at him and then dissolved into a broken doll. A boy screamed, "Abdu! Abdu!" Then redness filled his world. Hours passed, light and dark alternating at random.

It was Flinders who shook him awake this time. The afternoon sun had spread under the tent's edge. "Time to get up. You have been in bed for far too long. The shaykh expects us for the evening meal."

The prayers before dinner were long and solemn. The tent was crowded with men in long robes sitting cross-legged on mats. The meal was eaten in silence. Unayza served Pettigrew; her eyes never left his face.

After the trays were removed, the shaykh sighed and looked at his daughter. Then he leaned forward and touched Pettigrew on the shoulder. "I have spoken with my people, and we are one. We ask you to stay. You are one of us, Abul hol."

The shaykh studied Pettigrew's face. His eyes were worried.

"We must talk of happy things." The shaykh smiled. "You will become a great leader; men will sit at your feet to listen to your wisdom."

Again, he glanced at his daughter; his face was drawn. Unayza did not smile.

"You will have sons and daughters without number." He looked back at Pettigrew. "Your life will be full beyond measure."

Pettigrew did not move.

The shaykh smiled, but his eyes were sad. "We will laugh and pray and sing the old songs." He leaned close and put his hand on Pettigrew's shoulder. "My son, come with us."

The sitting men stopped moving. Flinders closed his eyes. Lawrence stared into space.

Pettigrew stared into the shaykh's eyes, and then he sat back. He could see Unayza standing behind her father. Her eyes were hidden in the shadow, but he sensed their question.

Now it comes. It should be so simple. Stay here and marry Unayza. Become the father to ten strong sons and daughters without number, all of them doting on their father. My tent would be full; my pasture would be alive with a hundred camels, and sheep beyond counting. A soft life . . . a good life.

He felt Unayza's eyes seek him out.

The tent waited in hushed silence. Pettigrew could hear the sands shifting in the night and the animals moving in their pens.

But I cannot stay.

"Besides," a voice spoke in his mind, "you are taken."

He turned to Lawrence. "Please translate. I am honored beyond words, but my heart is heavy. You are brothers and sisters to me. But I cannot stay. My destiny lies elsewhere. It was chosen long ago. It cannot be changed. Perhaps there is another, someone better, to be with you . . ." His voice trailed off.

Perhaps Lawrence will lead you.

As Lawrence translated, his voice shook.

Flinders sighed and slumped in his seat.

The shaykh nodded. "I sensed that you had another destiny. It is God's will—al-Qada wal Qadar. What will be, will be." The shaykh fingered his beads.

Pettigrew looked where Unayza had stood behind her father, but she was gone.

The dinner finished at last. Flinders and Pettigrew returned to their respective tents. Lawrence said good night. The camp was still. Moonlight sprayed across Pettigrew's hand as he lifted the tent flap. He looked back. The black cutouts of the tents were outlined in silver.

A world of starkness and shimmering light. What have I lost? She asked only that I love her and cherish her.

The cloth was rough to his fingers.

Nothing complex, just a simple relationship between a man and a woman.

A hint of spice from the dinner caught his nose.

She asked only that I love and laugh, that I hug and enjoy.

Somewhere a horse coughed in the still night.

But I am too complex, too "civilized" for such a relationship. I am a creature of my time.

He entered the tent; pale silver turned to black as the flap closed.

I am doomed to wander the world like a sailor who wanders at sea. Searching, searching, but never finding.

He sat on a cushion with his head in his hands. His hands were wet.

Morning light burned his eyes. Flinders said, "Coffee, my friend. We need to go. The car is ready—we must say our goodbyes."

Pettigrew dressed in his khakis.

These seem strange now, as though I am changing worlds.

He opened the flap and went outside. On the way out, he picked up the dagger. Its handle curved to his hand.

Will I never hold this blade again?

The car was in front of him, its engine running. Lawrence and Flinders were already seated, and the shaykh stood outside the car. Pettigrew shook the shaykh's hand.

The shaykh tapped his chest. "Maa Salama," he said. "Go in peace."

Women and children crowded around him.

"Ya, ya, Abul hol."

"Ya, ya, Abul hol."

The chants moved with him. As he walked, he brushed the hands that reached out.

I do not want to leave.

He saw her standing behind some children. She stepped forward. He saw a tear.

You have risked an honor killing to be with me. I am not worth it.

He remembered that he still held the dagger. He examined the blade; there was a large notch where it caught the saber. Lawrence had once translated the small inscription on its hilt: "Let the sword decide." His fingers closed between the two stars on the handle. He put it back in the sheath and handed it to her.

"Tell her this, please," he said, turning to Lawrence. "This blade saved my life, and so have you. I am forever indebted."

Lawrence spoke in Arabic and then nodded. "Well said."

Pettigrew got in. The leather seat squeaked, and the door closed with a final thump. The car started moving. Pettigrew turned in his seat. The black tents receded behind him. The women and children waving goodbye grew smaller. Men fired guns in the air, their smoke drifting up in lazy circles. There were many people. But he saw only one woman.

And she left me long ago.

The desert closed in, and the tents vanished in the shimmering heat.

ELEVEN

All Men Dream, but Not Equally

The wind was cold; the sea was cold; the railing was cold.

He was cold. Gravel crunched under his feet. "She's just down that path," the old attendant had said and pointed with his cane. Sunlight bounced off the pebbles as he walked. The white markers of the Greek cemetery seemed to watch him. At the end of the path, he saw a small Union Jack. There was a headstone, and he knelt to read its writing.

Pettigrew leaned over the railing and contemplated the waves rippling by the steamer's hull. The greens and blues folded into each other, their crests sparkling in the sun. The chug of the engines lulled him. He rubbed his shoulder. His mind wandered. Ghosts of smiles floated by his eyes; faint voices reached his ears.

I will remember these people and these places for the rest of my life. They may disappear, but they will live forever in my being.

He stretched and rubbed his eyes.

It was a time of wonder. The sounds of the empire will always echo down the corridors of my mind.

A gull squawked by. Pettigrew watched it swoop and flap until it disappeared into the distance.

The shriek of a desert hawk circling alone in the emptiness.
Its wings were black against the bright sun.
The loneliness of the desert will always touch me in the day and in the night.
He looked up.
Yes, it was a time of wonder.
The sun slid behind a cloud; the brightness dimmed.
The headstones turned from pink to gray as the sun set. The warm Cairo air became cold. The mourners had left, their shadows slanted across the gravel paths as they walked. The small Union Jack fluttered beside the marble. He was alone and cold. He wondered if Sami was cold also.

He spread his hands on the railing. The sparkling waves became a sullen gray. The bright splashes faded.
The world turns dark.
He stayed in the wetness for a while and then turned and went into his cabin.

The voyage was long and uneventful. Then, with a series of proud honks, the steamer docked. Flinders and Pettigrew loaded their luggage into a cab and got in. The cab smelled of wet wool; it splashed along the streets. A stray band of sunlight brightened the sky.
Maybe there is hope.
But the band of light faded and the rain began.

The museum was shadowy in the rain. Gusts of fog circled its columns. Streetlights had just come on, circles of light in gauzy rings that stretched away into the dark. The cab pulled up to the curb, and they got out. Flinders told the driver to wait. In his arms, wrapped in dirty canvas, he held the precious relic that had taken so much from them. Pettigrew followed.
So small to have cost so much.

The air smelled of wet grass as they passed the lush lawn and climbed the broad stairs. Pettigrew looked up as they went under the foyer. The Greek horses pranced above him.

They approached the bronze doors, and Flinders hammered on them. After a moment, one opened a crack, and a face peered out.

"Eunice," Flinders exclaimed, "how good to see you."

A door swung wide.

She dropped the broom she was holding. Her mouth opened and formed an "o."

"My goodness, it's the detectives." She covered her face with her hand. "I was just cleanin' the lobby when I heard the banging."

Then she stared. "Lardy, you both look so thin and tan."

"Is Director Budge still here?"

Eunice shook her head. "No, but his assistant is working late." She motioned for them to come. I'll show you to his office—it's down this hall."

They walked down a long hall. Eunice trotted ahead of them. Boxes and crates were stacked on each side. An occasional sarcophagus tilted against the green wall. Marble arms and legs littered the floor. Bodiless Greek heads smiled at them. They reached a door.

"This is the assistance's office." Eunice curtsied and left.

They knocked. The door opened. A man came out.

The assistant was a small man with flowing white hair and enormous muttonchops—he was every inch a curator. Pettigrew detected a sweet cologne.

"Director Budge left suddenly for Alexandria," he informed them. "A new bust of Cleopatra has been discovered." The assistant turned. "He received your cable and thanks you profusely." He pointed. "His office is just there. Follow me."

The small plaque read KEEPER OF ANTIQUITIES. The assistant unlocked the door. Stale cigar smoke wafted out. Pettigrew looked in. Precision was everywhere: Books on shelves stood at attention. Papers marched in close order on tables. An old tweed jacket with leather elbow patches hung on a hall tree. A half-empty bottle of claret stood sentry on a shelf. Two glasses sat next to it; one still had dregs in it.

He never washed it after Old George died.

Flinders carefully placed the soiled package on the polished desktop. "Our mission is complete."

The assistant locked the door. "I will have a guard posted." He shook their hands. Pettigrew noticed a tear wander down his cheek and disappear into the muttonchops. "The director thanks you. The museum thanks you. The world thanks you. And I thank you. It is such a relief." The assistant's jaw quivered.

"It was our pleasure."

"And by the way," Flinders grinned. "If you have any other such problems, please do call on us."

Flinders, there is no stopping you, is there?

They turned to leave. A large gray cat appeared from nowhere and rubbed against Pettigrew's leg.

"What is this?"

"Her name is Lois. She is the director's new cat. She guards the museum at night. The director is quite fond of her. Every morning, he feeds her and talks to her. She lies on his desk for the rest of the day while he works."

"Indeed." Pettigrew laughed. "And I suppose that the director cuddles her when he thinks you are not watching."

"How did you guess?"

"You forget that I am a detective."

Flinders added, "A long time ago, we had a discussion with the director about cats. I am sure that he is most protective of Lois."

Most protective, indeed.

They returned to the waiting cab. "And now let us go home." Flinders opened the cab door. The hinges squeaked.

They squeaked in Istanbul, too.

The cab splashed to a stop. The driver put their luggage on the curb and then drove off in a cloud of exhaust. They stepped onto the sidewalk.

Pettigrew saw that nothing had changed. The black door glistened. Drops ran down the lettering of the bronze plaque. Flinders spread his hands to catch the rain.

"I have missed this."

Maggie confronted them at the door. "You know how I worry about you when you go off to these awful places." She pulled them into the hallway. She brushed away a tear. "Just look at you—you look like ragamuffins. Come in, come in. You will catch your death of cold." She peered into their faces. "Goodness, gracious, your noses are sunburned. I will get some ointment." They walked down the hall and took off their overcoats. Their shoes left small puddles on the polished floor. Maggie frowned in disapproval. "Now off you go to get cleaned up. Mind you don't make a mess. And don't come back until you look like gentlemen."

Every time we come home, you cluck and fuss over us. You tear off our wet clothes and put ointment on our sunburned noses. Then you banish us to get cleaned up while you cook mutton. Could anyone ask for more?

They climbed the narrow stairs and walked down the hallway. Sarah Bernhardt dressed as Cleopatra smiled from her playbill. Pettigrew smiled at the sight.

"Cleopatra, you come at us in many guises."

In many guises, but they are all the same; they all hark back to some past before time began. We did not know who you were in Cairo, and we do not know who you are now. All we can do is to experience your being.

They cleaned up as instructed and returned to the dining room. It was warm and unchanged; the oak table gleamed with crystal and silver, and the decanter and glasses stood ready on the sideboard. The fat birds flew around the walls. The white-curtained window was covered in mist, and the smell of cooking mutton wafted up from the kitchen. Flinders looked around. Two men in suits solemnly stared at him from their golden frame. He saluted the portrait.

"It is good to be home."

"Yes, it is good to be home."

The sailor finally comes home from the sea.

Pettigrew poured two glasses of cognac and began humming "Flow Gently Sweet Afton."

Flinders joined in. The song grew louder. Pettigrew raised his glass.

I am home, but am I home? What have I given up to be here?

"To us."

"Yes, to us, and to the Serpent Woman."

They drank. Then silence for a moment. Flinders put his glass down.

"Shall we continue as detectives?"

"We have had this discussion before."

"I know. The issues are the same."

Flinders put his elbows on the table. "What we do has consequences. We solve a crime, and there is a hanging."

"It cannot be helped."

Flinders folded his napkin. "It is a heavy burden. Holmes solved it by everything being an intellectual puzzle. But he knew."

Pettigrew leaned back in his chair. "We decided that long ago."

And we are condemned to suffer the consequences.

Flinders put his hands on the table and stared at them. "Thomas, I feel that I am condemned to wander the earth. I must always search for the far pavilions. I must always go beyond one horizon to the next horizon."

"You have just come back from an adventure."

"I am driven."

"You have always been driven. Even at Oxford. I remember the light in your eyes when you burst through the door with that flyer about Bell's lectures. The thought of adventure was all over you."

"Are we all driven?"

"Yes, but for us there is a terrible cost." Pettigrew raised his glass and then set it down. "We have chosen our destiny. We are alone in the world. We are cut off from family and friends. We are like the Dutchman in the legend. We are condemned to sail the seas forever and always be haunted by memories of what might have been."

Sami smiled at me once. Her smile hangs in the air before me now.

"Then Holmes has had the last laugh."

"Indeed, he has." Pettigrew stared at the empty glass.

"We have lost our souls."

"We lost them in Egypt years ago."

We lost them when we descended into the tomb. We searched for Cleopatra in the underground, like Osiris searching for his lost Isis.

"So you think that we should continue?" Flinders poured himself another cognac.

"Of course we should."

"You are sure?"

"Yes." Pettigrew sat back and pushed the empty glass away. The Medusa face on its stem was impassive. "Yes, I am sure."

"The world is changing."

"And so are we."

Flinders swirled his cognac. "You do not think that we have become too old?"

"Too old?" Pettigrew was surprised by the question. "Flinders, I never expected you to worry about growing old."

"Yes, I do." Flinders touched the gray at his temples. "There is more of this each time I look in the mirror."

We are more alike than I imagined.

"That thought occurred as I saw the Bulbul's sword coming at me." Pettigrew grimaced. "But mind you, no more wall climbing, and no more camels."

"Nonsense! You were magnificent." Flinders laughed. "You climbed, you rode, and you swung a sword." He stopped and thought for a moment. "By the way, I did not know that you could fence. How did you learn to handle that sword? I thought that savate was your forte."

Pettigrew smiled and poured another glass. "While you were charming the ladies at school, I took broadsword lessons. With all modesty, I must say that I became very adept. I kept it up ever since."

"Indeed." Flinders held his glass up to the light. "What do you think about Lawrence and Gertrude?"

Pettigrew put his elbows on the table. "What do I think? I think that they are all creatures of their past demons. It is as if they have death wishes. They do not care what happens to them. I imagine that Lawrence will risk danger once too often—he will race down one road too many. And Gertrude will die by her own hand quietly and at night."

Flinders put his glass down. "You have become a philosopher, my friend. But I suspect you have always been one."

"Maybe so." Pettigrew frowned into his glass. "Lawrence has suffered some terrible injury as a boy. He will project it on the landscape. The world of the bedouin is his stage. He may yet have his desert war. We will hear more from him."

"And Gertrude."

Pettigrew sighed. "A girl who grew up searching for an impossible love. She will displace her loneliness onto the Middle East. Her energy will dominate the area. But she will never be happy." Pettigrew stared at his glass. "I will miss those green eyes."

"When we boarded the steamer, I saw the captain hand you a note."

"It was from Gertrude," Pettigrew said. "But I would rather not discuss it."

"I understand."

But he had read it to himself, over and over, until it was seared into his memory. It was only a few lines.

Thomas,
When you read this, I shall be far away. I once said, "The desert
is like an opal."
But that opal is you.
Love,
Gertrude

He had folded the letter and stared into space. Then he put it in a drawer. Flinders spoke. "And Kudret?"

"Kudret . . ." Pettigrew swirled the cognac. "A complex man with a complex life. Taken as a boy, trained in the arts of seduction, and then transformed into an intelligence master. A man terribly hurt, but a man who overcame it. A man who dreams of a golden past but who sees his dream fading before his eyes. He can do nothing but watch." Pettigrew took a sip. "His koceks and his tulips, everything that he loves, have begun to disappear before him. He swam in a sea of exquisite custom, a sea of elaborate distinction. Now that sea is drying up. For him, the old ways, like the old headgear, will be lost. How terrible."

"Our world is fading as well."

"You feel it coming also?" Pettigrew held up his glass. The lamplight glimmered through Medusa's face. "If only you could talk, what secrets you could tell."

Flinders nodded. "And Unayza?"

"Unayza . . ." Pettigrew put the glass down and placed his head in his hands. "Once before you asked me a hard question; now you ask a second."

"Thomas . . ." Flinders stopped and examined the floor.

Pettigrew covered his face. "Another world. A world of warmth . . . a world of discipline . . . a world of honor and prayer and goodness. But also a vanishing world." His eyes teared. "They walk, long shadows, into the dusty sunset. Soon nothing will be left of them but solemn images that look out of tattered photographs."

He poured another glass and took a sip. "I was tempted, Flinders, terribly tempted"—he stared at the glass—"to leave this world and enter that other world. To vanish with Unayza and with them. But my own demons prevented that."

"Indeed." Flinders nodded. "We all have demons."

"I once said that I was a man of science. Cold, hard facts were my altar." He held the glass to the light. "But now I don't know. In our quest for scientific 'truth,' we may have given up our humanness." He took another sip. "In our quest for knowledge, we may have become isolated from one another." He drank. "The mystery of life disappears before our eyes."

"You have become an anarchist railing at modern civilization."

Pettigrew laughed. "Kudret said that he drank too much, and now I join him."

Both our worlds are fading as though with the end of a bright sunlit day.

"And the Veiled One?"

"I suspect that we will meet him again face-to-face."

"His presence looms over us."

Pettigrew contemplated the caramel depths of his glass. "The Veiled One is like the jinn. Flinders, do you remember what Woolley said? 'Jinns are creatures of ancient evil. They change shapes to confuse humans, and they rampage without mercy.'"

"He was speaking of pre-Islamic legends about an invisible people."

"Are we so sure that there is not an unknown darkness beyond our comprehension?"

Am I so sure that this unknown darkness does not come from within?

"I do not know."

"Jinns were made of smoke and fire," Pettigrew said. "The Veiled One was born in fire, and he will die in fire."

"So now you are a prophet?"

"No, I am only a middle-aged detective. We are not done with the Veiled One. I can feel it in my bones." Pettigrew frowned. "This jinn will return."

And so will we.

"I agree."

Flinders poured another glass. "So now we are here."

"Yes, we are here."

"And what do we face?"

"A cataclysm," Pettigrew said. "You told me that they were preparing for war."

"They seemed quite eager to get on with it."

"Indeed, they are."

Flinders smoothed his hair. "But the end is not yet."

"No, the end is not yet."

They sat for a moment in silence and then returned to the sitting room. Cleopatra looked down. Isis smiled from her pedestal—a knowing smile. The room was unchanged. Letters overflowed the small chinoiserie table. Pettigrew shuffled the stack. Letters fell on the floor. Flinders picked up a letter.

"Ah, English Violet. Excellent taste."

Then he put the letter down and stared into space. "But there was another perfume."

He went to the window. "I wonder." He parted the curtains. "I wonder if I shall ever smell it again." Fog clouded the window. "Or ever see the woman who wears it."

Pettigrew heard the words, and his thoughts went back to a time when the sun was beginning to set.

He leaned close to see the inscription better. The letters were blurred before his eyes.

In memory of Sami Papadopoulos,
wife, mother, and loyal servant of the Crown
Though we die, yet shall we live.

Pettigrew sighed and picked up another perfumed letter. "That perfume smells atrocious." Pettigrew sniffed the letter. "We shall have to open the window."

He put it down and held up an envelope. "Wait. What is this? It is from a Miss Bara." Pettigrew handed it to Flinders. He thought a moment and then grinned. "Didn't we meet her before we left?" He laughed. "Ah yes, the actress. Something about a silver screen, I believe. Flinders, how much champagne did you give that woman?"

Flinders opened the envelope and took out a letter written on pink stationery.

"She said that the Americans are making films in a place called Hollywood."

"Hollywood? What is Hollywood? Is it a forest of some kind?"

"No, it is a city." Flinders opened the envelope. "We could make a film about the desert."

"The desert?"

"Yes, about a shaykh in the desert."

"A shaykh in the desert." Pettigrew stroked his chin. "That will never happen."

"Just think," Flinders said, brushing the objection aside. "We could cross on the *Titanic*."

"The *Titanic*? It is still a shipbuilder's dream. Besides, I would get seasick."

"A shipbuilder's dream. We all have dreams."

"The trick is to make them real."

"All men dream," Lawrence had said, "but not equally."

Flinders shrugged and reached across the mantel. "Someone has sent us a gift."

A packet tied together with an envelope was on it. Flinders opened the envelope, read the contents, and laughed. "Budge has paid us . . . and handsomely, too. Let us see what is in the packet." He broke the string and tore it open. "Aha! These are very fine cigars! They will go excellently with cognac. Thomas, try one."

Pettigrew took the cigar and held it under his nose. "Very fine, indeed." He struck a match.

The sitting room door burst open, and Maggie flew in. "Stop where you are! If I have told you once, I have told you a thousand times—you cannot smoke those filthy things in my house. Out you go, out into the garden! Out. Out. Out." She trundled them out of the sitting room, down the back stairs, and pushed them through the garden door. "Now, don't come back in until you are done. I have mutton cooking for your dinner."

They went into the garden.

Pettigrew sat on the bench, and Flinders sat on the sphinx. Both lit their cigars. Neither spoke. A light rain, really a mist, fell on them. The garden smelled of wet roses. Cigar smoke swirled and outlined the two figures with pale clouds. Occasional dots of red glowed and faded in the soft darkness.

I loved you, so I drew these tides of
Men into my hands
And wrote my will across the
Sky and stars
—T. E. Lawrence, *Seven Pillars of Wisdom*

About the Author

John Amos holds a PhD from the University of California at Berkeley and a JD from the Monterey College of Law. He has taught at university level for twenty-five years. His academic publications include two books, *Arab-Israeli Military/Political Relations: Arab Perceptions and the Politics of Escalation* and *Palestinian Resistance: Organization of a Nationalist Movement*, as well as numerous articles in major academic journals. He is also a coeditor of *Gulf Security into the 1980s: Perceptual and Strategic Dimensions*. His fiction works include *The Student* (2022), *The Cleopatra Caper* (2023), and *The Charge* (forthcoming). He has lived in the Middle East, most notably in Egypt, Lebanon, Libya, and Turkey. He currently practices law.

Made in the USA
Las Vegas, NV
02 May 2024

89391037R00132